FLAXMAN LOW

The Radium Age Book Series
Joshua Glenn

Voices from the Radium Age, edited and introduced by Joshua Glenn, 2022
A World of Women, J. D. Beresford, 2022
The World Set Free, H. G. Wells, 2022
The Clockwork Man, E. V. Odle, 2022
Nordenholt's Million, J. J. Connington, 2022
Of One Blood, Pauline Hopkins, 2022
What Not, Rose Macaulay, 2022
The Lost World and The Poison Belt, Arthur Conan Doyle, 2023
Theodore Savage, Cicely Hamilton, 2023
The Napoleon of Notting Hill, G. K. Chesterton, 2023
The Night Land, William Hope Hodgson, 2023
More Voices from the Radium Age, edited and introduced by Joshua Glenn, 2023
Man's World, Charlotte Haldane, 2024
The Inhumans and Other Stories: A Selection of Bengali Science Fiction, edited and translated by Bodhisattva Chattopadhyay, 2024
The People of the Ruins, Edward Shanks, 2024
The Heads of Cerberus and Other Stories, Francis Stevens, edited and introduced by Lisa Yaszek, 2024
The Greatest Adventure, John Taine, 2025
The Hampdenshire Wonder, J. D. Beresford, 2025
Before Superman: Superhumans of the Radium Age, edited and introduced by Joshua Glenn, 2025
Yankees in Petrograd, Marietta S. Shaginyan, translated and introduced by Jill Roese, 2025
Flaxman Low: Occult Detective, E. and H. Heron, edited and introduced by Alexander B. Joy, 2026
Beatrice the Sixteenth, Irene Clyde, 2026

PRAISE FOR THE RADIUM AGE SERIES

"New editions of a host of under-discussed classics of the genre."
—*Reactor Magazine*

"Neglected classics of early 20th-century sci-fi in spiffily designed paperback editions."
—*Financial Times*

"An entertaining, engrossing glimpse into the profound and innovative literature of the early twentieth century."
—*Foreword*

"Shows that 'proto-sf' was being published much more widely, alongside other kinds of fiction, before it emerged as a genre."
—*BSFA Review*

"An excellent start at showcasing the strange wonders offered by the Radium Age."
—*Shelf Awareness*

"Lovingly curated . . . The series' freedom from genre purism lets us see how a specific set of anxieties—channeled through dystopias, Lovecraftian horror, arch social satire, and adventure tales—spurred literary experimentation and the bending of conventions."
—*Los Angeles Review of Books*

"A huge effort to help define a new era of science fiction."
—*Transfer Orbit*

"Admirable . . . and highly recommended."
—*Washington Post*

"Long live the Radium Age."
—*Los Angeles Times*

FLAXMAN LOW

OCCULT DETECTIVE

E. and H. Heron

edited and introduced by Alexander B. Joy

THE MIT PRESS
CAMBRIDGE, MASSACHUSETTS
LONDON, ENGLAND

The MIT Press
Massachusetts Institute of Technology
77 Massachusetts Avenue
Cambridge, MA 02139
mitpress.mit.edu

This edition of *Flaxman Low: Occult Detective* follows the text of the 1899 edition published by C. Arthur Pearson Ltd., which is in the public domain.

This book was set in Arnhem Pro and PF DIN Text Pro by New Best-set Typesetters Ltd. Printed and bound in the United States of America.

Library of Congress Cataloging-in-Publication Data is available.

ISBN: 978-0-262-05165-1

10 9 8 7 6 5 4 3 2 1

EU Authorised Representative: Easy Access System Europe, Mustamäe tee 50, 10621 Tallinn, Estonia | Email: gpsr.requests@easproject.com

CONTENTS

SERIES FOREWORD

Joshua Glenn

Do we really know science fiction? There were the scientific romance years that stretched from the mid-nineteenth century to circa 1900. And there was the genre's so-called golden age, from circa 1935 through the early 1960s. But between those periods, and overshadowed by them, was an era that has bequeathed us such tropes as the robot (berserk or benevolent), the tyrannical superman, the dystopia, the unfathomable extraterrestrial, the sinister telepath, and the eco-catastrophe. In 2009, writing for the sf blog io9.com at the invitation of Annalee Newitz and Charlie Jane Anders, I became fascinated with the period during which the sf genre as we know it emerged. Inspired by the exactly contemporaneous career of Marie Curie, who shared a Nobel Prize for her discovery of radium in 1903, only to die of radiation-induced leukemia in 1934, I eventually dubbed this three-decade interregnum the "Radium Age."

Curie's development of the theory of radioactivity, which led to the extraordinary, terrifying, awe-inspiring insight that the atom is, at least in part, a state of energy constantly in movement, is an apt metaphor for the twentieth century's first three decades. These years were marked by rising sociocultural strife across various fronts: the founding of the women's suffrage movement, the

National Association for the Advancement of Colored People, socialist currents within the labor movement, anticolonial and revolutionary upheaval around the world . . . as well as the associated strengthening of reactionary movements that supported, for example, racial segregation, immigration restriction, eugenics, and sexist policies.

Science—as a system of knowledge, a mode of experimenting, and a method of reasoning—accelerated the pace of change during these years in ways simultaneously liberating and terrifying. As sf author and historian Brian Stableford points out in his 1989 essay "The Plausibility of the Impossible," the universe we discovered by means of the scientific method in the early twentieth century defies common sense: "We are haunted by a sense of the impossibility of ultimately making sense of things." By playing host to certain far-out notions—time travel, faster-than-light travel, and ESP, for example—that we have every reason to judge impossible, science fiction serves as an "instrument of negotiation," Stableford suggests, with which we strive to accomplish "the difficult diplomacy of existence in a scientifically knowable but essentially unimaginable world." This is no less true today than during the Radium Age.

The social, cultural, political, and technological upheavals of the 1900–1935 period are reflected in the proto-sf writings of authors such as Olaf Stapledon, William Hope Hodgson, Muriel Jaeger, Karel Čapek, G. K. Chesterton, Cicely Hamilton, W. E. B. Du Bois, Yevgeny Zamyatin, E. V. Odle, Arthur Conan Doyle, Mikhail Bulgakov, Pauline

Hopkins, Stanisław Ignacy Witkiewicz, Aldous Huxley, Gustave Le Rouge, A. Merritt, Rudyard Kipling, Rose Macaulay, J. D. Beresford, J. J. Connington, S. Fowler Wright, Jack London, Thea von Harbou, and Edgar Rice Burroughs, not to mention the late-period but still incredibly prolific H. G. Wells himself. More cynical than its Victorian precursor yet less hard-boiled than the sf that followed, in the writings of these visionaries we find acerbic social commentary, shock tactics, and also a sense of frustrated idealism—and reactionary cynicism, too—regarding humankind's trajectory.

The MIT Press's Radium Age series represents a much-needed evolution of my own efforts to champion the best proto-sf novels and stories from 1900 to 1935 among scholars already engaged in the fields of utopian and speculative fiction studies, as well as general readers interested in science, technology, history, and thrills and chills. By reissuing literary productions from a time period that hasn't received sufficient attention for its contribution to the emergence of science fiction as a recognizable form—one that exists and has meaning in relation to its own traditions and innovations, as well as within a broader ecosystem of literary genres, each of which, as John Rieder notes in *Science Fiction and the Mass Cultural Genre System* (2017), is itself a product of overlapping "communities of practice"—we hope not only to draw attention to key overlooked works but perhaps also to influence the way scholars and sf fans alike think about this crucial yet neglected and misunderstood moment in the emergence of the sf genre.

John W. Campbell and other Cold War–era sf editors and propagandists dubbed a select group of writers and story types from the pulp era to be the golden age of science fiction. In doing so, they helped fix in the popular imagination a too-narrow understanding of what the sf genre can offer. (In his introduction to the 1974 collection *Before the Golden Age*, for example, Isaac Asimov notes that although it may have possessed a certain exuberance, in general sf from before the mid-1930s moment when Campbell assumed editorship of *Astounding Stories* "seems, to anyone who has experienced the Campbell Revolution, to be clumsy, primitive, naive.") By returning to an international tradition of scientific speculation via fiction from after the Poe–Verne–Wells era and before sf's Golden Age, the Radium Age series will demonstrate—contra Asimov et al.—the breadth, richness, and diversity of the literary works that were responding to a vertiginous historical period, and how they helped innovate a nascent genre (which wouldn't be named until the mid-1920s, by Hugo Gernsback, founder of *Amazing Stories* and namesake of the Hugo Awards) as a mode of speculative imagining.

The MIT Press's Noah J. Springer and I are grateful to the sf writers and scholars who have agreed to serve as this series' advisory board. Aided by their guidance, we'll endeavor to surface a rich variety of texts, along with introductions by a diverse group of sf scholars, sf writers, and others that will situate these remarkable, entertaining, forgotten works within their own social, political, and scientific contexts, while drawing out contemporary parallels.

We hope that reading Radium Age writings, published in times as volatile as our own, will serve to remind us that our own era's seemingly natural, eternal, and inevitable social, economic, and cultural forms and norms are—like Madame Curie's atom—forever in flux.

INTRODUCTION: ALL IS NATURAL

Alexander B. Joy

Psychological science once broke ground in asserting that there were physical, material reasons behind the processes of the mind. Until Wilhelm Wundt began to teach scientific psychology in the 1860s, psychology was regarded as merely a branch of philosophy, but psychologists worldwide would follow Wundt in setting up laboratories for the scientific study of mind and behavior. By the 1890s, the decade at the end of which the stories collected in this volume were first published, it was becoming widely accepted that the brain and its chemistry governs our movements, emotions, thoughts, and mental states. From out of this seismic theoretical shift emerges Flaxman Low, the hero of these stories.

"Flaxman Low" is the pseudonym of a gentlemanly, athletic psychological researcher with an unusual specialty: ghosts and the paranormal. Beleaguered petitioners seek him out to diagnose all kinds of odd and troubling occurrences; his unflappable competence in the presence of ghostly terrors makes him seem as if he may already have one foot in the spirit world. Low represents perhaps the first truly modern "occult detective," an archetypal weird fiction figure who investigates, and sometimes eradicates, seemingly supernatural or mystical phenomena—though only after establishing a scientific basis for their occurrence.

Up until Low, occult mysteries either reject the paranormal outright, or else they embrace a paranormal completely untethered from physical laws. Sherlock Holmes, for example, never entertains supernatural prospects: "The world is big enough for us. No ghosts need apply," he quips in the 1924 adventure "The Sussex Vampire." L.T. Meade's and John Eustace's John Bell (protagonist of an 1896 story collection, *A Master of Mysteries*) offers an earlier example of ghost-themed mysteries, but his quests involve disproving the supernatural. And while Sheridan Le Fanu's Dr. Hesselius (from the 1872 collection *In a Glass Darkly*) also researches the paranormal, the causes and cures he turns up are typically fantastical.

What distinguishes Low from conventional detectives and credulous proto-occult detectives alike, and what makes him a pioneer who paved the way for Algernon Blackwood's John Silence, William Hope Hodgson's Thomas Carnacki, and many other occult detectives since, is a willingness to ascribe supernatural occurrences to psychological causes—and therefore to consider such causes fair game as possible solutions to a number of mysteries.

The furtherance of psychological science furnishes both the ethos and the high concept behind Low's adventures. "We [scientific psychologists] stand to-day on the frontier of an unknown world," he declares in his first outing, "and progress is the result of individual effort; each solution of difficult phenomena forms a step towards the solution of the next problem." Low's stories use the still-nascent discipline as a springboard for a series of speculative mystery and horror stories, exploring the peculiarities of the human mind as our hero probes real and imagined ghost sightings, stress- and chemical-induced hallucinations, mental projections that occupy space (or take over other beings), and consciousness that persists after death.

These adventures make for entertaining reads on their own merits. Their evocative settings range from picturesque English mansions to sweeping Old World countrysides to the coast of Calais. Their psychological (sub)text often rivals the depth and disquiet of Henry James's ghost stories. (As in James's 1898 gothic horror novella *The Turn of the Screw*, for example, the specter of molestation tacitly hangs over "The Story of Medhans Lea.") Low's exploits also feature a number of memorably bizarre set pieces, including a disinterred earth demon that inherits a cough from the terminally ill person that it unwittingly consumes, an Egyptian mummy piloted by a vampire, and a preserved human body that has morphed into a phosphorescent mushroom mannequin after a mycological revenge scheme gone awry.

If this sounds less like science fiction than "weird fiction," that's because the former genre developed to some extent out of the latter during science fiction's emergent Radium Age (c. 1900–1935). The boundary between the genres was permeable; what helped differentiate science fiction was a certain empirical, inductive approach to knowledge-making. Emily Alder, editor of the journal *Gothic Studies*, places the Flaxman Low stories in the latter grouping in her 2020 study *Weird Fiction and Science at the Fin de Siècle*: "Low's explanations arguably contain and neutralise weirdness," i.e., by fixing what is otherwise unexplainable within a tractable, intelligible framework—and dispensing with its threats accordingly. As Low himself summarizes the stories' driving philosophy: "You know I hold that there is no such thing as the supernatural; all is natural."

"Flaxman Low" was the brainchild of British author Kate O'Brien Prichard and her son Hesketh Hesketh-Prichard. Under the collective pseudonym "E. and H. Heron," they published the adventures collected here in two series in *Pearson's Magazine* in 1898 and 1899; these were then collected in book form, in 1899, as *Ghosts: Being the Experiences of Flaxman Low*.

Hesketh, nicknamed "Hex," led a fascinating if brief life in which he played cricket at a professional level, overhauled the standard training regimen for British Army snipers, and traveled the world as a newspaper correspondent. Kate, daughter of a notable military family, was also a great traveler, often joining Hex on his assignments. (The Rio Caterina, in what is now Argentina's Parque Nacional Los Glaciares, is named for her.) The Prichards wrote a number of popular, well-received novels and stories, including *A Modern Mercenary* (1898), *The Chronicles of Don Q* (1904), and *Don Q's Love Story* (1909); the latter would be adapted into the 1925 Douglas Fairbanks vehicle *Don Q, Son of Zorro*.

Regarding the Flaxman Low tales, the Prichards' exact division of labor is disputed. The science fiction and fantasy scholar Everett F. Bleiler credits Hesketh as "the major partner in their collaborations," whereas Eric Parker, in his 1924 memoir about Hesketh, hints that Kate may have exerted directorial influence. Hesketh himself gives Kate considerable deference in a *Pearson's* introduction to his work from July 1903: "I owe everything [. . .] to my mother. She has helped me with all that I have written, and without her I should probably have written nothing." Stylistic variations among the Flaxman Low stories may suggest that a single Prichard took the lead in writing each story, though the series overall can be attributed more or less equally to both Prichards.

The Prichards were acquainted with many major figures of their day, including J. M. Barrie and Arthur Conan Doyle. If Flaxman Low was one of many fictional detectives rushed into print to fill the Sherlock-shaped void after Conan Doyle's "The Final Problem" (1893) seemingly offed the author's wildly popular creation, the influence may have run in both directions. In travel writer Bruce Chatwin's influential first book, *In Patagonia* (1977), for example, Chatwin suggests that Hex Prichard's popular 1902 travelog *Through the Heart of Patagonia* "seems to have been an ingredient of Conan Doyle's [1912 proto-sf novel] *The Lost World*."

Like *The Lost World* and other stories from the era in which British imperialism is taken for granted, there are respects in which the Flaxman Low stories betray their age. For example, anti-Chinese racism inflects "The Story of № 1 Karma Crescent," surfacing in Low's disdainful descriptions of the local immigrant population's clothing. In "The Story of Konnor Old House," meanwhile, a character refers to a man from Africa using a vile slur; Low himself identifies the same man using then-proper but now-dated language. The many casual allusions to Britain's empire found throughout these stories suggest that the series is well-suited for postcolonial analysis; "The Story of Konnor Old House," in particular, begs for a postcolonial reading.

Let's hope that such reappraisal includes appreciation for Flaxman Low's legacy. Echoes of the Prichards' stories persist throughout horror, mystery, and sci-fi—especially where those genres combine. The Low stories offered proofs-of-concept as to how effectively these genres might meld; their influence can be detected from H. P. Lovecraft through Thomas Ligotti. Low's psychologically oriented methods and insatiable curiosity make him a precursor to memorable investigators such as G. K. Chesterton's Father Brown and Fox Mulder of *The X-Files*.

Psychological science (and its congeners that, in hindsight, were pseudoscience) saw a number of significant developments in the late 1800s. The ideas and principles behind them were firmly ensconced in the popular imagination by the time the Prichards wrote these stories.

In 1882, the Society for Psychical Research (which still exists today) was founded in England to conduct formal inquiries into what would now be dismissed as "the paranormal" and "parapsychology," but was once dubbed "psychical science." In its heyday, the SPR's ranks included serious scientists and philosophers. The SPR's American cousin, the (also still extant) American Society for Psychical Research, appeared in 1884, with noted psychologist

William James as a founding member. James went on to publish the influential *The Principles of Psychology* in 1890, which established the premise and promise of psychological science: to pin thoughts, feelings, and mental states to physical parts or conditions of the brain. Meanwhile, Sigmund Freud's psychoanalytic methods and frameworks also came to prominence in the 1890s, which laid the early groundwork for methodological and clinical approaches to the mind.

The Flaxman Low tales, several of which place Low in Vienna during Freud's productive periods, and others of which name him among the Society for Psychical Research's regular contributors, portray their protagonist as conversant with the psychological science of the era. The unique metafictional presentation of the stories' initial print run underscores this "realistic" context. *Pearson's* billed Low's adventures as "real ghost stories," and to lend credence to the investigations each was accompanied by "actual photographs" of the haunted houses.

Their packaging speaks to the hopes underpinning the stories' late Victorian context: If science could more clearly understand the mind and brain, then souls and spirits—as artifacts of the brain's formerly nebulous mechanisms—might likewise evolve from myth into fact. These stories therefore see Low attempting to furnish logical explanations for subject matter that formerly belonged to fantasy alone, by "approach[ing] the elucidation of so-called supernatural problems on the lines of natural law" (per the introductory note), and "deal[ing] with these mysterious affairs as far as possible on material lines" (as Low says in "The Story of Yand Manor House"). Whereas psychological science had opened the possibility that matters of mind and spirit are as beholden to the tangible and physical as the rest of the body, the Flaxman Low stories offered imaginative explorations of this possibility's potential consequences.

The protagonist of the stories in this book treads a middle path between skepticism and receptivity, persuasively insisting that any solution to a mystery is possible . . . and in such a fashion arrives at ingenious paranormal and nonparanormal solutions. (The latter range from identifying living impostors to discovering potent airborne toxins that cause people to perceive what isn't there.) There is always a rational, scientific explanation to hand: "[T]here are no other laws in what we term the realm of the supernatural," Low says in "The Story of Konnor Old House," "but those which are the projections or extensions of natural laws."

The Flaxman Low stories are as much about expanding the purview of psychology as shrinking the domain of the inexplicable, thus transforming the unknowable into the understood.

Further Reading

Alder, Emily. *Weird Fiction and Science at the Fin de Siècle*. Cham, Switzerland: Palgrave Macmillan, 2020.

Bleiler, Everett F. *The Guide to Supernatural Fiction*. Kent, OH: The Kent State University Press, 1983.

Chatwin, Bruce. *In Patagonia*. New York: Penguin, 2003.

Parker, Eric. *Hesketh Prichard: A Memoir*. New York: E. P. Dutton and Company, 1924.

INTRODUCTION

The following is an extract from a letter dated February 1896, and addressed to the authors:—

"... I think I may say that I am the first student in this field of inquiry who has had the boldness to break free from the old and conventional methods, and to approach the elucidation of so-called supernatural problems on the lines of natural law.

"Have ghosts any existence outside our own fancy and emotion? This is the question with which the end of the century concerns itself more and more, for, though a vast amount of evidence with regard to occult phenomena already exists, the ultimate answer has yet to be supplied. In this connection it may not generally be known that, as one of the first steps towards reducing Psychology to the lines of an exact science, an attempt has been made to classify spirits and ghosts, with the result that some very bizarre and terrible theories have been put forward—things undreamt of outside the circle of the select few.

"My object in sending you these notes is that you may (should you think fit) prepare from them some sort of volume of a popular character. In case this suggestion should fall in with your ideas, will you undertake the task?

"All that I ask is that you should disguise my identity, as I have no wish to pose as a fanatic, and with this stipulation I leave the matter in your hands, and remain, very truly yours,

"FLAXMAN LOW."

AUTHORS' NOTE.—The following pages are the outcome of that letter of Mr. Flaxman Low's. And let us here say that, beyond that letter and the notes therein referred to, Mr. Low has had no connection with or responsibility for these stories. The proof-sheets were never submitted to him, as before the MS. was completed Mr. Low had disappeared into the wilderness of West Africa on that expedition to which he refers in these pages. So for any mistakes, or *errata*, the authors must be held solely responsible.

THE STORY OF "THE SPANIARDS," HAMMERSMITH

Lieutenant Roderick Houston, of H.M.S. *Sphinx*, had practically nothing beyond his pay, and he was beginning to be very tired of the West African station, when he received the pleasant intelligence that a relative had left him a legacy. This consisted of a satisfactory sum in ready money and a house in Hammersmith, which was rated at over £200 a year, and was said in addition to be comfortably furnished. Houston, therefore, counted on its rental to bring his income up to a fairly desirable figure. Further information from home, however, showed him that he had been rather premature in his expectations, whereupon, being a man of action, he applied for two months' leave, and came home to look after his affairs himself.

When he had been a week in London, he arrived at the conclusion that he could not possibly hope single-handed to tackle the difficulties which presented themselves. He accordingly wrote the following letter to his friend, Flaxman Low:—

"The Spaniards," Hammersmith, 23-3-1892.

"DEAR LOW,—Since we parted some three years ago, I have heard very little of you. It was only yesterday that I met our mutual friend, Sammy Smith ("Silkworm" of our schooldays), who told me that your studies have developed in a new direction, and that you are now a good deal interested in psychical subjects. If this be so, I hope to induce you to come and stay with me here for a few days by promising to introduce you to a problem in your own line. I am just now living at 'The Spaniards,' a house that has lately been left to me, and which in the first instance was built by an old fellow named Van Nuysen, who married a great-aunt of mine. It is a good house, but there is said to be 'something wrong' with it. It lets easily, but unluckily the tenants cannot be persuaded to remain above a week or two. They complain that the place is haunted by something—presumably a ghost—because its vagaries bear just that brand of inconsequence which stamps the common run of manifestations.

"It occurs to me that you may care to investigate the matter with me. If so, send me a wire when to expect you.—Yours ever, RODERICK HOUSTON."

Houston waited in some anxiety for an answer. Low was the sort of man one could rely on in almost any emergency. Sammy Smith had told him a characteristic anecdote of Low's career at Oxford, where, although his intellectual triumphs may be forgotten, he will always be remembered by the story that when Sands, of Queen's, fell ill on the day before the 'Varsity sports, a telegram was sent to Low's rooms: "Sands ill. You must do the hammer for us." Low's reply was pithy: "I'll be there." Whereupon he finished the treatise upon which he was engaged, and next day his strong, lean figure was to be seen swinging the hammer amidst vociferous cheering, for that was the occasion on which he not only won the event, but beat the record.

On the fifth day Low's answer came from Vienna. As he read it, Houston recalled the high forehead, long neck—with its accompanying low collar—and thin moustache of his scholarly, athletic friend, and smiled. There was so much more in Flaxman Low than any one had been inclined to give him credit for in the old days:—

"MY DEAR HOUSTON,—Very glad to hear of you again. In response to your kind invitation, I thank you for the opportunity of meeting the ghost, and still more for the pleasure of your companionship. I came here to inquire into a somewhat similar affair. I hope, however, to be able to leave to-morrow, and will be with you sometime on Friday evening.—Very sincerely yours,

FLAXMAN LOW.

"*P.S.*—By the way, will it be convenient to give your servants a holiday during the term of my visit, as, if my investigations are to be of any value, not a grain of dust must be disturbed in your house, excepting by ourselves?—F. L."

"The Spaniards" was within some fifteen minutes' walk of Hammersmith Bridge. Set in the midst of a fairly respectable neighbourhood it presented an odd contrast to the commonplace dulness of the narrow streets crowded about it. As Flaxman Low drove up in the evening light, he reflected that the house might have come from the back of beyond—it gave an impression of something old-world and something exotic.

It was surrounded by a ten-foot wall, above which the upper story was visible, and Low decided that this intensely English house still gave some curious suggestion of the tropics. The interior of the building carried out the same idea, with its sense of space and air, cool tints and wide-matted passages.

"So you have seen something yourself since you came?" Low said, as they sat at dinner, for Houston had arranged that meals should be sent in for them from a hotel.

"I've heard tapping up and down the passage upstairs. It is an uncarpeted landing which runs the whole length of the house. One night, when I was quicker than usual, I saw what looked like a bladder disappear into one of the bedrooms—your room it is to be, by the way—and the door closed behind it," replied Houston discontentedly. "The usual meaningless antics of a ghost."

"What had the tenants who lived here to say about it?" went on Low.

"Most of the people saw and heard just what I have told you, and promptly went away. The only one who stood out for a little while was old Filderg—you know the man? Twenty years ago he made an effort to cross the Australian deserts. He stopped for eight weeks. When he left he saw the house-agent, and said he was afraid he had done a little shooting practice in the upper passage, and he hoped it wouldn't count against him in the bill, as it was in defence of his life. He said something had jumped onto the bed and tried to strangle him. He described it as cold and glutinous, and he pursued it down the passage, firing at it. He advised the owner to have the house pulled down; but, of course, my cousin, the then owner, did nothing of the kind. It's a very good house, and he did not see the sense of spoiling his property."

"That's very true," replied Flaxman Low, looking round. "Mr. Van Nuysen had been in the West Indies, and kept his liking for spacious rooms."

"Where did you hear anything about him?" asked Houston in surprise.

"I have heard nothing beyond what you told me in your letter; but I see a couple of bottles of Gulf-weed and a lace-plant ornament, such as people used to bring from the West Indies in former days."

"Perhaps I should tell you the history of the old man," said Houston doubtfully; "but we aren't proud of it!"

Flaxman Low considered a moment.

"When was the ghost seen for the first time?"

"When the first tenant took the house. It was let after old Van Nuysen's time."

"Then it may clear the way if you will tell me something of him."

"He owned sugar plantations in Trinidad, where he passed the greater part of his life, while his wife mostly remained in England—incompatibility of temper it was said. When he came home for good and built this house they still lived apart, my aunt declaring that nothing on earth would persuade her to return to him. In course of time he became a confirmed invalid, and he then insisted on my aunt joining him. She lived here for perhaps a year, when she was found dead in bed one morning—in your room."

"What caused her death?"

"She had been in the habit of taking narcotics, and it was supposed that she smothered herself while under their influence."

"That doesn't sound very satisfactory," remarked Flaxman Low.

"Her husband was satisfied with it anyhow, and it was no one else's business. The family were only too glad to have the affair hushed up."

"And what became of Mr. Van Nuysen?"

"That I can't tell you. He disappeared a short time after. Search was made for him in the usual way, but nobody knows to this day what became of him."

"Ah, that was strange, as he was such an invalid," said Low, and straightway fell into a long fit of abstraction, from which he was roused by hearing Houston curse the incurable foolishness and imbecility of ghostly behaviour. Flaxman woke up at this. He was a man with an immense capacity for quiet enthusiasm. He broke a walnut thoughtfully, and began in a gentle voice—

"My dear fellow, we are apt to be hasty in our condemnation of the general behaviour of ghosts. It may appear incalculably foolish in our eyes, and I admit there often seems to be a total absence of any apparent object or intelligent action. But remember that what appears to us to be foolishness may be wisdom in the spirit-world, since our unready senses can only catch broken glimpses of what is, I have not the slightest doubt, a coherent whole, if we could trace the connection."

"There may be something in that," replied Houston indifferently. "People naturally say that this ghost is the ghost of old Van Nuysen. But what connection can possibly exist between what I have told you of him and the manifestations—a tapping up and down the passage and the drawing about of a bladder like a child at play? It sounds idiotic!"

"Certainly. Yet it need not necessarily be so. These are isolated facts; we must look for the links which lie between. Suppose a saddle and a horse-shoe were to be shown to a man who had never seen a horse, I doubt whether he, however intelligent, could evolve the connecting idea! The ways of spirits are strange to us simply because we need further data to help us to interpret them."

"It's a new point of view," returned Houston, "but upon my word, you know, Low, I think you're wasting your time!"

Flaxman Low smiled slowly; his grave, melancholy face brightened.

"I have," said he, "gone somewhat deeply into the subject. In other sciences one reasons by analogy. Psychology is unfortunately a science with a future but without a past, or more probably it is a lost science of the ancients. However that may be, we stand to-day on the frontier of an unknown world, and progress is the result of individual effort; each solution of difficult phenomena forms a step towards the solution of the next problem. In this case, for example, the bladder-like object may be the key to the mystery."

Houston yawned.

"It all seems pretty senseless, but perhaps you may be able to read reason into it. If it were anything tangible, anything a man could meet with his fists, it would be easier."

"I entirely agree with you. But suppose we deal with this affair as it stands, on similar lines, I mean on prosaic, rational lines, as we should deal with a purely human mystery."

"My dear fellow," returned Houston, pushing his chair back from the table wearily, "you shall do just as you like, only get rid of the ghost!"

For some time after Low's arrival nothing very special happened. The tappings continued, and more than once Low had been in time to see the bladder disappear into the closing door of his bedroom, but however quickly he followed the bladder, he never succeeded in seeing anything further. He made a thorough examination of the house, and left no space unaccounted for in his careful measurements. There were no cellars, and the foundation of the house consisted of a thick layer of concrete.

At length, on the sixth night, an event took place, which, as Flaxman Low remarked, came very near to putting an end to the investigations so far as he was concerned. For the preceding two nights he and Houston had kept watch in the hope of getting a glimpse of the person or thing which tapped so persistently up and down the passage. But they were disappointed, for there were no manifestations. On the third evening, therefore, Low went off to his room a little earlier than usual, and fell asleep almost immediately.

He says he was awakened by feeling a heavy weight upon his feet, something that seemed inert and motionless. He recollected that he had left the gas burning, but the room was now in darkness.

Next he was aware that the thing on the bed had slowly shifted, and was gradually travelling up towards his chest.

How it came on the bed he had no idea. Had it leaped or climbed? The sensation he experienced as it moved was of some ponderous, pulpy body, not crawling or creeping, but spreading! It was horrible! He tried to move his lower limbs, but could not because of the deadening weight. A feeling of drowsiness began to overpower him, and a deadly cold, such as he said he had before felt at sea when in the neighbourhood of icebergs, chilled upon the air.

With a violent struggle he managed to free his arms, but the thing grew more irresistible as it spread upwards. Then he became conscious of a pair of glassy eyes, with livid, everted lids, looking into his own. Whether they were human eyes or beast eyes he could not tell, but they were watery, like the eyes of a dead fish, and gleamed with a pale, internal lustre.

Then he owns he grew afraid. But he was still cool enough to notice one peculiarity about this ghastly visitant—although the head was within a few inches of his own, he could detect no breathing. It dawned upon him that he was about to be suffocated, for, by the same method of extension, the thing was now coming over his face! It felt cold and clammy, like a mass of mucilage or a monstrous snail. And every instant the weight became greater. He is a powerful man, and he struck with his fists again and again at the head. Some substance yielded under the blows with a sickening sensation of bruised flesh.

With a lucky twist he raised himself in the bed and battered away with all the force he was capable of in his cramped position. The only effect was an occasional shudder or quake that ran through the mass as his half-arm blows rained upon it. At last, by chance, his hand knocked against the candle beside him. In a moment he recollected the matches. He seized the box, and struck a light.

As he did so, the lump slid to the floor. He sprang out of bed, and lit the candle. He felt a cold touch upon his leg, but when he looked down there was nothing to be seen. The door, which he had locked overnight, was now open, and he rushed out into the passage. All was still and silent with the throbbing vacancy of night-time.

After searching round, he returned to his room. The bed still gave ample proof of the struggle that had taken place, and by his watch he saw the hour to be between two and three.

As there seemed nothing more to be done, he put on his dressing-gown, lit his pipe, and sat down to write an account of the experience he had just passed through for the Psychical Research Society—from which paper the above is an abstract.

He is a man of strong nerves, but he could not disguise from himself that he had been at handgrips with some grotesque form of death. What might be the nature of his assailant he could not determine, but his experience was supported by the attack which had been made on Filderg, and also—it was impossible to avoid the conclusion—by the manner of Mrs. Van Nuysen's death.

He thought the whole situation over carefully in connection with the tapping and the disappearing bladder, but, turn these events how he would, he could make nothing of them. They were entirely incongruous. A little later he went and made a shakedown in Houston's room.

"What was the thing?" asked Houston, when Low had ended his story of the encounter.

Low shrugged his shoulders.

"At least it proves that Filderg did not dream," he said.

"But this is monstrous! We are more in the dark than ever. There's nothing for it but to have the house pulled down. Let us leave to-day."

"Don't be in a hurry, my dear fellow. You would rob me of a very great pleasure; besides, we may be on the verge of some valuable discovery. This series of manifestations is even more interesting than the Vienna mystery I was telling you of."

"Discovery or not," replied the other, "I don't like it."

The first thing next morning Low went out for a quarter of an hour. Before breakfast a man with a barrowful of sand came into the garden. Low looked up from his paper, leant out of the window, and gave some order.

When Houston came down a few minutes later he saw the yellowish heap on the lawn with some surprise.

"Hullo! What's this?" he asked.

"I ordered it," replied Low.

"All right. What's it for?"

"To help us in our investigations. Our visitor is capable of being felt, and he or it left a very distinct impression on the bed. Hence I gather it can also leave an impression on sand. It would be an immense advance if we could arrive at any correct notion of what sort of feet the ghost walks on. I propose to spread a layer of this sand in the upper passage, and the result should be footmarks if the tapping comes to-night."

That evening the two men made a fire in Houston's bedroom, and sat there smoking and talking, to leave the ghost "a free run for once," as Houston phrased it. The tapping was heard at the usual hour, and presently the accustomed pause at the other end of the passage and the quiet closing of the door.

Low heaved a long sigh of satisfaction as he listened.

"That's my bedroom door," he said; "I know the sound of it perfectly. In the morning, and with the help of daylight, we shall see what we shall see."

As soon as there was light enough for the purpose of examining the footprints, Low roused Houston.

Houston was as full of excitement as a boy, but his spirits fell by the time he had passed from end to end of the passage.

"There are marks," he said, "but they are as perplexing as everything else about this haunting brute, whatever it is. I suppose you think this is the print left by the thing which attacked you the night before last?"

"I fancy it is," said Low, who was still bending over the floor eagerly. "What do you make of it, Houston?"

"The brute has only one leg, to start with," replied Houston, "and that leaves the mark of a large, clawless pad! It's some animal—some ghoulish monster!"

"On the contrary," said Low, "I think we have now every reason to conclude that it is a man."

"A man? What man ever left footmarks like these?"

"Look at these hollows and streaks at the sides; they are the traces of the sticks we have heard tapping."

"You don't convince me," returned Houston doggedly.

"Let us wait another twenty-four hours, and to-morrow night, if nothing further occurs, I will give you my conclusions. Think it over. The tapping, the bladder, and the fact that Mr. Van Nuysen had lived in Trinidad. Add to these things this single pad-like print. Does nothing strike you by way of a solution?"

Houston shook his head.

"Nothing. And I fail to connect any of these things with what happened both to you and Filderg."

"Ah! now," said Flaxman Low, his face clouding a little, "I confess you lead me into a somewhat different region, though to me the connection is perfect."

Houston raised his eyebrows and laughed.

"If you can unravel this tangle of hints and events, and diagnose the ghost, I shall be extremely astonished," he said. "What can you make of the footless impression?"

"Something, I hope. In fact, that mark may be a clue—an outrageous one, perhaps, but still a clue."

That evening the weather broke, and by night the storm had risen to a gale, accompanied by sharp bursts of rain.

"It's a noisy night," remarked Houston; "I don't suppose we'll hear the ghost, supposing it does turn up."

This was after dinner, as they were about to go into the smoking-room. Houston, finding the gas low in the hall, stopped to turn it higher, at the same time asking Low to see if the jet on the upper landing was also alight.

Flaxman Low glanced up and uttered a slight exclamation, which brought Houston to his side.

Looking down at them from over the banisters was a face—a blotched, yellowish face, flanked by two swollen, protruding ears, the whole aspect being strangely leonine. It was but a glimpse, a clash of meeting glances, as it were, a glare of defiance, and the face was quickly withdrawn as the two men literally leapt up the stairs.

"There's nothing here," exclaimed Houston, after a search had been carried out through every room above.

"I didn't suppose we'd find anything," returned Low.

"This fairly knots up the thread," said Houston. "You can't pretend to unravel it now."

"Come down," said Low briefly; "I am ready to give you my opinion, such as it is."

Once in the smoking-room, Houston busied himself in turning on all the light he could procure, then he saw to securing the windows, and piled up an immense fire, while Flaxman Low, who, as usual, had a cigarette in his mouth, sat on the edge of the table and watched him with some amusement.

"You saw that abominable face?" cried Houston, as he threw himself into a chair. "It was as material as yours or mine. But where did he go to? He must be somewhere about."

"We saw him clearly. That is sufficient for our purpose."

"You are very good at enumerating points, Low. Now just listen to my list. The difficulties grow with every fresh discovery. We're at a deadlock now, I take it? The sticks and the tapping point to an old man, the playing with a bladder to a child; the footmark might be the pad of a tiger minus claws, yet the thing that attacked you at night was cold and pulpy. And, lastly, by way of a wind-up, we see a lion-like, human face! If you can make all these items square with each other, I'll be happy to hear what you have got to say."

"You must first allow me to ask you a question. I understood you to say that no blood relationship existed between you and old Mr. Van Nuysen?"

"Certainly not. He was quite an outsider," answered Houston brusquely.

"In that case you are welcome to my conclusions. All the things you have mentioned point to one explanation. This house is haunted by the ghost of Mr. Van Nuysen, and he was a leper."

Houston stood up and stared at his companion.

"What a horrible notion! I must say I fail to see how you have arrived at such a conclusion."

"Take the chain of evidence in rather different order," said Low. "Why should a man tap with a stick?"

"Generally because he's blind."

"In cases of blindness, one stick is used for guidance. Here we have two for support."

"A man who has lost the use of his feet."

"Exactly; a man who has from some cause partially lost the use of his feet."

"But the bladder and the lion-like face?" went on Houston.

"The bladder, or what seemed to us to resemble a bladder, was one of his feet, contorted by the disease, and probably swathed in linen, which foot he dragged rather than used; consequently, in passing through a door, for example, he would be in the habit of drawing it in after him. Now, as regards the single footmark we saw. In one form of leprosy, the smaller bones of the extremities frequently fall away. The pad-like impression was, as I believe, the mark of the other foot—a toeless foot which he used, because in a more advanced stage of the disease the maimed hand or foot heals and becomes callous."

"Go on," said Houston; "it sounds as if it might be true. And the lion-like face I can account for myself. I have been in China, and have seen it before in lepers."

"Mr. Van Nuysen had been in Trinidad for many years, as we know, and while there he probably contracted the disease."

"I suppose so. After his return," added Houston, "he shut himself up almost entirely, and gave out that he was a martyr to rheumatic gout, this awful thing being the true explanation."

"It also accounts for Mrs. Van Nuysen's determination not to return to her husband."

Houston appeared much disturbed.

"We can't drop it here, Low," he said, in a constrained voice. "There is a good deal more to be cleared up yet. Can you tell me more?"

"From this point I find myself on less certain ground," replied Low unwillingly. "I merely offer a suggestion, remember—I don't ask you to accept it. I believe Mrs. Van Nuysen was murdered."

"What?" exclaimed Houston. "By her husband?"

"Indications tend that way."

"But, my good fellow——"

"He suffocated her and then made away with himself. It is a pity that his body was not recovered; but, as his whole line of action proves that he was extremely sensitive on the subject of his disease, and very desirous to keep the matter a secret, it was to be expected that he would contrive some form of self-destruction which secured concealment of his dead body. I am inclined to believe that he murdered his wife because she was the sole sharer of his secret. However that may be, the condition of the remains would be the only really satisfactory test of my theory. If the skeleton could even now be found, the fact that he was a leper would be finally settled."

There was a prolonged pause until Houston put another question.

"Wait a minute, Low," he said. "Ghosts are admittedly immaterial. In this instance our spook has an extremely palpable body. Surely this is rather unusual? You have made everything else more or less plain. Can you tell me why this dead leper should have tried to murder you and old Filderg? And also how he came to have the actual physical power to do so?"

Low removed his cigarette to look thoughtfully at the end of it. "Now I lapse into the purely theoretical," he answered. "Cases have been known where the assumption of diabolical agency is apparently justifiable."

"Diabolical agency?—I don't follow you."

"I will try to make myself clear, though the subject is still in a stage of vagueness and immaturity. Van Nuysen committed a murder of exceptional atrocity, and afterwards killed himself. Now, bodies of suicides are known to be peculiarly susceptible to spiritual influences, even to the point of arrested corruption. Add to this our knowledge that the highest aim of an evil spirit is to achieve incarnation. If I carried out my theory to its logical conclusion, I should say that Van Nuysen's body is hidden somewhere on these premises—that this body is intermittently animated by some spirit, which at certain periods is forced to re-enact the gruesome tragedy of the Van Nuysens. Should any living person chance to occupy the position of the first victim, so much the worse for him!"

For some minutes Houston made no remark on this singular expression of opinion.

"But have you ever met with anything of the sort before?" he said at last.

"I can recall," replied Flaxman Low, thoughtfully, "quite a number of cases which would seem to bear out this hypothesis. Among them a curious problem of haunting exhaustively examined by Busner in the early part of 1888, at which I was myself lucky enough to assist. Indeed, I may add that the affair which I recently have been engaged upon in Vienna offers some rather similar features. There, however, we had to stop short of excavation, by which alone any specific results might have been attained."

"Then you are of the opinion," said Houston, "that pulling the house to pieces might cast some further light upon this affair?"

"I cannot see any better course," said Mr. Low.

Then Houston closed the discussion with a very definite declaration.

"This house shall come down!"

So "The Spaniards" was pulled down.

Such is the story of "The Spaniards," Hammersmith, and it has been given the first place in this series because, although it may not be of so strange a nature as some that will follow it, yet it seems to us to embody in a high degree the peculiar methods by which Mr. Flaxman Low is wont to approach these cases.

The work of demolition, begun at the earliest possible moment, did not occupy very long, and during its early stages, under the boarding at an angle of the landing was found a skeleton. Several of the phalanges were missing, and other indications also established beyond a doubt the fact that the remains were the remains of a leper. The space within which the bones lay had evidently been prepared by Van Nuysen for his purpose, the boards covering it being furnished with bolts on the underside by means of which he could fix them in position above him while lying at full length in the cavity between the beams below.

The skeleton is now in the museum of one of our city hospitals. It bears a scientific ticket, and is the only evidence extant of the correctness of Mr. Flaxman Low's methods and the possible truth of his extraordinary theories.

THE STORY OF MEDHANS LEA

The following story has been put together from the account of the affair given by Nare-Jones, sometime house-surgeon at Bart's, of his strange terror and experiences both in Medhans Lea and the pallid avenue between the beeches; of the narrative of Savelsan, of what he saw and heard in the billiard-room and afterwards; of the silent and indisputable witness of big, bullnecked Harland himself; and, lastly, of the conversation which subsequently took place between these three men and Mr. Flaxman Low, the noted psychologist.

It was by the merest chance that Harland and his two guests spent that memorable evening of the 18th of January 1889 in the house of Medhans Lea. The house stands on the slope of a partially wooded ridge in one of the Midland counties. It faces south, and overlooks a wide valley bounded by the blue outlines of the Bredon hills. The place is secluded, the nearest dwelling being a small public-house at the cross-roads some mile and a half from the lodge gates.

Medhans Lea is famous for its long straight avenue of beeches, and for other things. Harland, when he signed the lease, was thinking of the avenue of beeches; not of the other things, of which he knew nothing until later.

Harland had made his money by running tea plantations in Assam, and he owned all the virtues and faults of a man who has spent most of his life abroad. The first time he visited the house he weighed seventeen stone, and ended most of his sentences with "don't yer know?" His ideas could hardly be said to travel on the higher planes of thought, and his chief aim in life was to keep himself down to the seventeen stone. He had a red neck and a blue eye, and was a muscular, inoffensive, good-natured man, with courage to spare, and an excellent voice for accompanying the banjo.

After signing the lease, he found that Medhans Lea needed an immense amount of putting in order and decorating. While this was being done, he came backwards and forwards to the nearest provincial town, where he stopped at a hotel, driving out almost daily to superintend the arrangements of his new habitation. Thus he had been away for the Christmas and New Year, but about the 15th January he returned to the Red Lion, accompanied by his friends Nare-Jones and Savelsan, who proposed to move with him into his new house during the course of the ensuing week.

The immediate cause of their visit to Medhans Lea on the evening of the 18th inst. was the fact that the billiard-table at the Red Lion was not fit, as Harland remarked, to play shinty on, while there was an excellent table just put in at Medhans Lea, where the big billiard-room in the left wing had a wide window with a view down a portion of the beech avenue.

"Hang it!" said Harland, "I wish they would hurry up with the house. The painters aren't out of it yet, and the people don't come to the lodge till Monday."

“It’s a pity, too,” remarked Savelsan regretfully, “when you think of that table.”

Savelsan was an enthusiast in billiards, who spent all the time he could spare from his business, which happened to be tea-broking, at the game. He was the more sorry for the delay, since Harland was one of the few men he knew to whom it was not necessary to give points.

“It’s a ripping table,” returned Harland. “Tell you what,” he added, struck by a happy idea, “I’ll send out Thoms to make things straight for us to-morrow, and we’ll put a case of syphons and a bottle of whisky under the seat of the trap, and drive over for a game after dinner.”

The other two agreed to this arrangement, but in the morning Nare-Jones found himself obliged to run up to London to see about securing a berth as ship’s doctor. It was settled, however, that on his return he was to follow Harland and Savelsan to Medhans Lea.

He got back by the 8.30, entirely delighted, because he had booked a steamer bound for the Persian Gulf and Karachi, and had gained the cheering intelligence that a virulent type of cholera was lying in wait for the advent of the Mecca pilgrims in at any rate two of the chief ports of call, which would give him precisely the experience he desired.

Having dined, and the night being fine, he ordered a dogcart to take him out to Medhans Lea. The moon had just risen by the time he reached the entrance to the avenue, and as he was beginning to feel cold, he pulled up, intending to walk to the house. He dismissed the boy and cart, a carriage having been ordered to come for the whole party after midnight. Nare-Jones stopped to light a cigar before entering the avenue, then he walked past the empty lodge. He moved briskly, in the best possible temper with himself and all the world. The night was still, and his collar up, his feet fell silently on the dry carriage road, while his mind was away on blue water, forecasting his voyage on the s.s. *Sumatra*.

He says he was quite half-way up the avenue before he became conscious of anything unusual. Looking up at the sky, he noticed what a bright, clear night it was, and how well defined the outline of the beeches against the vault of heaven. The moon was yet low, and threw netted shadows of bare twigs and branches on the road, which ran between black lines of trees in an almost straight vista up to the dead grey face of the house, now barely two hundred yards away. Altogether, it struck him as forming a pallid picture, etched in, like a steel engraving, in black, and grey, and white.

He was thinking of this when he was aware of words spoken rapidly in his ear, and he turned, half expecting to see some one behind him. No one was visible. He had not caught the words, nor could he define the voice; but a vague conviction of some horrible meaning fixed itself in his consciousness.

The night was very still, ahead of him the house glimmered grey and shuttered in the moonlight. He shook himself, and walked on, oppressed by a novel sensation compounded of disgust and childish fear; and still, from behind his shoulder, came the evil, voiceless murmuring.

He admits that he passed the end of the avenue at an amble, and was abreast of a semicircle of shrubbery, when a small object was thrust out from the shadow of the bushes, and lay in the open light. Though the night was peculiarly still, it fluttered and balanced a moment, as if windblown, then came in skimming flights to his feet. He picked it up and made for the door, which yielded to his hand, and he flung it to and bolted it behind him.

Once in the warmly-lit hall his senses returned, and he waited to recover breath and composure before facing the two men whose voices and laughter came from a room on his right. But the door of the room was thrown open, and the burly figure of Harland in his shirt sleeves appeared on the threshold.

"Hullo, Jones, that you? Come along!" he said genially.

"Bless me!" exclaimed Nare-Jones irritably, "there's not a light in any of the windows. It might be a house of the dead!"

Harland stared at him, but all he said was: "Have a whisky-and-soda?"

Savelsan, who was leaning over the billiard-table trying side-strokes, with his back to Nare-Jones, added—

"Did you expect us to illuminate the place for you? There's not a soul in the house but ourselves."

"Say when," said Harland, poising the bottle over a glass.

Nare-Jones laid down what he held in his hand on the corner of the billiard-table, and took up his glass.

"What in creation's this?" asked Savelsan.

"I don't know; the wind blew it to my feet just outside," replied Nare-Jones, between two long pulls at the whisky-and-soda.

"*Blown* to your feet?" repeated Savelsan, taking up the thing and weighing it in his hand. "It must be blowing a hurricane then."

"It isn't blowing at all," returned Nare-Jones blankly. "The night is dead calm."

For the object that had fluttered and rolled so lightly across the turf and gravel was a small, battered, metal calf, made of some heavy brass amalgam.

Savelsan looked incredulously into Nare-Jones's face, and laughed.

"What's wrong with you? You look queer."

Nare-Jones laughed too; he was already ashamed of the last ten minutes.

Harland was meantime examining the metal calf.

"It's a Bengali idol," he said. "It's been knocked about a good bit, by Jove! You say it blew out of the shrubbery?"

"Like a bit of paper, I give you my word, though there was not a breath of wind going," admitted Nare-Jones.

"Seems odd, don't yer know?" remarked Harland carelessly. "Now you two fellows had better begin: I'll mark."

Nare-Jones happened to be in form that night, and Savelsan became absorbed in the delightful difficulty of giving him a sound thrashing.

Suddenly Savelsan paused in his stroke.

"What the sin's that?" he asked.

They stood listening. A thin, broken crying could be heard.

"Sounds like green plover," remarked Nare-Jones, chalking his cue.

"It's a kitten they've shut up somewhere," said Harland.

"That's a child, and in a deuce of a fright, too," said Savelsan. "You'd better go and tuck it up in its little bed, Harland," he added, with a laugh.

Harland opened the door. There could no longer be any doubt about the sounds; the stifled shrieks and thin whimpering told of a child in the extremity of pain or fear.

"It's upstairs," said Harland. "I'm going to see."

Nare-Jones picked up a lamp and followed him.

"I stay here," said Savelsan, sitting down by the fire.

In the hall the two men stopped and listened again. It is hard to locate a noise, but this seemed to come from the upper landing.

"Poor little beggar!" exclaimed Harland, as he bounded up the staircase. The bedroom doors opening on the square central landing above were all locked, the keys being on the outside. But the crying led them into a side passage which ended in a single room.

"It's in here, and the door's locked," said Nare-Jones. "Call out and see who's there."

But Harland was set on business. He flung his weight against the panel, and the door burst open, the lock ricocheting noisily into a corner. As they passed in, the crying ceased abruptly.

Harland stood in the centre of the room, while Nare-Jones held up the light to look round.

"The dickens!" exclaimed Harland exhaustively.

The room was entirely empty.

Not so much as a cupboard broke the smooth surface of the walls, only the two low windows and the door by which they had entered.

"This is the room above the billiard-room, isn't it?" said Nare-Jones at last.

"Yes. This is the only one I have not had furnished yet. I thought I might——"

He stopped short, for behind them burst out a peal of harsh, mocking laughter, that rang and echoed between the bare walls.

Both men swung round simultaneously, and both caught a glimpse of a tall, thin figure in black, rocking with laughter in the doorway, but when they turned it was gone. They dashed out into the passage and landing. No one was to be seen. The doors were locked as before, and the staircase and hall were vacant.

After making a prolonged search through every corner of the house, they went back to Savelsan in the billiard-room.

"What were you laughing about? What is it anyway?" began Savelsan at once.

"It's nothing. And we didn't laugh," replied Nare-Jones definitely.

"But I heard you," insisted Savelsan. "And where's the child?"

"I wish you'd go up and find it," returned Harland grimly. "We heard the laughing and saw, or thought we saw, a man in black——"

"Something like a priest in a cassock," put in Nare-Jones.

"Yes, like a priest," assented Harland, "but as we turned he disappeared."

Savelsan sat down and gazed from one to the other of his companions.

"The house behaves as if it was haunted," he remarked; "only there is no such thing as an authenticated ghost outside the experiences of the Psychical Research Society. I'd ask the Society down if I were you, Harland. You never can tell what you may find in these old houses."

"It's not an old house," replied Harland. "It was built somewhere about '40. I certainly saw that man; and, look to it, Savelsan, I'll find out who or what he is. That I swear! The English law makes no allowance for ghosts—nor will I."

"You'll have your hands full, or I'm mistaken," exclaimed Savelsan, grinning. "A ghost that laughs and cries in a breath, and rolls battered idols about your front door, is not to be trifled with. The night is young yet—not much past eleven. I vote for a peg all round and then I'll finish off Jones."

Harland, sunk in a fit of sullen abstraction, sat on a settee, and watched them. On a sudden he said—

"It's turned beastly cold."

"There's a beastly smell, you mean," corrected Savelsan crossly, as he went round the table. He had made a break of forty and did not want to be interrupted. "The draught is from the window."

"I've not noticed it before this evening," said Harland, as he opened the shutters to make sure.

As he did so the night air rushed in heavy with the smell as of an old well that has not been uncovered for years, a smell of slime and unwholesome wetness. The lower part of the window was wide open and Harland banged it down.

"It's abominable!" he said, with an angry sniff. "Enough to give us all typhoid."

"Only dead leaves," remarked Nare-Jones. "There are the rotten leaves of twenty winters under the trees and outside this window. I noticed them when we came over on Tuesday."

"I'll have them cleared away to-morrow. I wonder how Thoms came to leave this window open," grumbled Harland, as he closed and bolted the shutter. "What do you say—forty-five?" and he went over to mark it up.

The game went on for some time, and Nare-Jones was lying across the table with the cue poised, when he heard a slight sound behind him. Looking round he saw Harland, his face flushed and angry, passing softly—wonderfully softly for so big a man, Nare-Jones remembers thinking—along the angle of the wall towards the window.

All three men unite in declaring that they were watching the shutter, which opened inwards as if thrust by some furtive hand from outside. At the moment Nare-Jones and Savelsan were standing directly opposite to it on the further side of the table, while Harland crouched behind the shutter intent on giving the intruder a lesson.

As the shutter unfolded to its utmost the two men opposite saw a face pressed against the glass, a furrowed evil face, with a wide laugh perched upon its sinister features.

There was a second of absolute stillness, and Nare-Jones's eyes met those other eyes with the fascinated horror of a mutual understanding, as all the foul fancies that had pursued him in the avenue poured back into his mind.

With an uncontrollable impulse of resentment, he snatched a billiard-ball from the table and flung it with all his strength at the face. The ball crashed through the glass and through—the face beyond it! The glass fell shattered, but the face remained for an instant peering and grinning at the aperture, then as Harland sprang forward it was gone.

"The ball went clean through it!" said Savelsan with a gasp.

They crowded to the window, and throwing up the sash, leant out. The dank smell clung about the air, a boat-shaped moon glimmered between the bare branches, and on the white drive beyond the shrubbery the billiard ball could be seen a shining spot under the moon. Nothing more.

"What was it?" asked Harland.

"'Only a face at the window,'" quoted Savelsan with an awkward attempt at making light of his own scare. "Devilish queer face too, eh, Jones?"

"I wish I'd got him!" returned Harland frowning. "I'm not going to put up with any tricks about the place, don't yer know?"

"You'd bottle any tramp loafing round," said Nare-Jones.

Harland looked down at his immense arms outlined in his shirt-sleeves.

"I could that," he answered. "But this chap—did you hit him?"

"Clean through the face! or, at any rate, it looked like it," replied Savelsan, as Nare-Jones stood silent.

Harland shut the shutter and poked up the fire.

"It's a cursed creepy affair!" he said. "I hope the servants won't get hold of this nonsense. Ghosts play the very mischief with a house. Though I don't believe in them myself, don't yer know?" he concluded.

Then Savelsan broke out in an unexpected place.

"Nor do I—as a rule," he said slowly. "Still you know it is a sickening idea to think of a spirit condemned to haunt the scene of its crime waiting for the world to die."

Harland and Nare-Jones looked at him.

"Have a whisky neat," suggested Harland soothingly. "I never knew you taken that way before."

Nare-Jones laughed out. He says he does not know why he laughed nor why he said what follows.

"It's this way," he said. "The moment of foul satisfaction is gone for ever, yet for all time the guilty spirit must perpetuate its sin—the sin that brought no lasting reward, only a momentary reward experienced, it may be, centuries ago, but to which still clings the punishment of eternally rehearsing in loneliness, and cold, and gloom, the sin of other days. No punishment can be conceived more horrible. Savelsan is right."

"I think we've had enough about ghosts," said Harland cheerfully, "let's go on. Hurry up, Savelsan."

"There's the billiard ball," said Nare-Jones. "Who'll go fetch?"

"Not I," replied Savelsan promptly. "When that—was at the window, I felt sick."

Nare-Jones nodded. "And I wanted to bolt!" he said emphatically.

Harland faced about from the fire.

"And I, though I saw nothing but the shutter, I—hang it!—don't yer know—so did I! There was panic in the air for a minute. But I'm shot if I'm afraid now," he concluded doggedly. "I'll go."

His heavy animal face was lit with courage and resolution.

"I've spent close upon five thousand pounds over this blessed house first and last, and I'm not going to be done out of it by any infernal spiritualism!" he added, as he took down his coat and pulled it on.

"It's all in view from the window except those few yards through the shrubbery," said Savelsan. "Take a stick and go. Though, on second thoughts, I bet you a fiver you don't."

"I don't want a stick," answered Harland. "I'm not afraid—not now—and I'd meet most men with my hands."

Nare-Jones opened the shutters again; the sash was low, and he pushed the window up and leant far out.

"It's not much of a drop," he said, and slung his legs out over the lintel; but the night was full of the smell, and something else. He leapt back into the room. "Don't go, Harland!"

Harland gave him a look that set his blood burning.

"What is there, after all, to be afraid of in a ghost?" he asked heavily.

Nare-Jones, sick with the sense of his own newly-born cowardice, yet entirely unable to master it, answered feebly—

"I can't say, but don't go."

The words seemed inevitable, though he could have kicked himself for hanging back.

There was a forced laugh from Savelsan.

"Give it up and stop at home, little man," he said.

Harland merely snorted in reply, and laid his great leg over the window ledge. The other two watched his big, tweed-clad figure as it crossed the grass and disappeared into the shrubbery.

"You and I are in a preposterous funk," said Savelsan, with unpleasant explicitness, as Harland, whistling loudly, passed into the shadow.

But this was a point on which Nare-Jones could not bring himself to speak at that moment. Then they sat on the sill and waited. The moon shone out clearly above the avenue, which now lay white and undimmed between its crowding trees.

"And he's whistling because he's afraid," continued Savelsan.

"He's not often afraid," replied Nare-Jones shortly; "besides, he's doing what neither of us were very keen on."

The whistling stopped suddenly. Savelsan said afterwards that he fancied he saw Harland's huge, grey-clad shoulders, with uplifted arms, rise for a second above the bushes.

Then out of the silence came peal upon peal of that infernal laughter, and, following it, the thin, pitiful crying of the child. That too ceased, and an absolute stillness seemed to fall upon the place.

They leant out and listened intently. The minutes passed slowly. In the middle of the avenue the billiard-ball glinted on the gravel, but there was no sign of Harland emerging from the shrubbery path.

"He should be there by now," said Nare-Jones anxiously.

They listened again; everything was quiet. The ticking of Harland's big watch on the mantelpiece was distinctly audible.

"This is too much," said Nare-Jones. "I'm going to see where he is."

He swung himself out on the grass, and Savelsan called to him to wait, as he was coming also. While Nare-Jones stood waiting, there was a sound as of a pig grunting and rooting among the dead leaves in the shrubbery.

They ran forward into the darkness, and found the shrubbery path. A minute later they came upon something that tossed and snorted and rolled under the shrubs.

"Great Heavens!" cried Nare-Jones, "it's Harland!"

"He's breaking somebody's neck," added Savelsan, peering into the gloom.

Nare-Jones was himself again. The powerful instinct of his profession—the help-giving instinct, possessed him to the exclusion of every other feeling.

"He's in a fit—just a fit," he said in matter-of-fact tones, as he bent over the struggling form, "that's all."

With the assistance of Savelsan, he managed to carry Harland out into the open drive. Harland's eyes were fearful, and froth hung about his blue puffing lips as they laid him down upon the ground. He rolled over, and lay still, while from the shadows broke another shout of laughter.

"It's apoplexy. We must get him away from here," said Nare-Jones. "But, first, I'm going to see what is in those bushes."

He dashed through the shrubbery, backwards and forwards. He seemed to feel the strength of ten men as he wrenched and tore and trampled the branches, letting in the light of the moon to its darkness. At last he paused, exhausted.

"Of course, there's nothing," said Savelsan wearily. "What did you expect after the incident of the billiard-ball?"

Together, with awful toil, they bore the big man down the narrow avenue, and at the lodge gates they met the carriage.

*

Some time later the subject of their common experiences at Medhans Lea was discussed amongst the three men. Indeed, for many weeks Harland had not been in a state to discuss any subject at all, but as soon as he was allowed to do so, he invited Nare-Jones and Savelsan to meet Mr. Flaxman Low, the scientist, whose works on psychology and kindred matters are so well known, at the Métropole to thresh out the matter.

Flaxman Low listened with his usual air of gentle abstraction, from time to time making notes on the back of an envelope. He looked at each narrator in turn as he took up the thread of the story. He understood perfectly that the man who stood furthest from the mystery must inevitably have been the self-centred Savelsan; next in order came Nare-Jones, with sympathetic possibilities, but a crowded brain; closest of all would be big, kindly Harland, with more than one strong animal instinct about him, and whose bulk of matter was evidently permeated by a receptive spirit.

When they had ended, Savelsan turned to Flaxman Low.

"There you have the events, Mr. Low. Now, the question is how to deal with them."

"Classify them," replied Flaxman Low.

"The crying would seem to indicate a child," began Savelsan, ticking off the list on his fingers; "the black figure, the face at the window, and the laughter are naturally connected. So far I can go alone. I conclude that we saw the apparition of a man, possibly a priest, who had during his lifetime ill-treated a child, and whose punishment it is to haunt the scene of his crime."

"Precisely—the punishment being worked out under conditions which admit of human observation," returned Flaxman Low. "As for the child, the sound of crying was merely part of the *mise-en-scène*."

"But that explanation stops short of several points. How about the suggestive thoughts experienced by my friend Nare-Jones; what brought on the fit in the case of Mr. Harland, who assures us that he was not suffering from fright or other violent emotion; and what connection can be traced between all these things and the Bengali idol?" Savelsan ended.

"Let us take the Bengali idol first," said Low. "It is just one of those discrepant particulars which, at first sight, seem wholly irreconcilable with the rest of the phenomena, yet these often form a test point, by which our theories are proved or otherwise." Flaxman Low took up the metal calf from the table as he spoke. "I should be inclined to connect this with the child. Observe it. It has not been roughly used; it is rubbed and dinted as a plaything usually is. I should say the child may have had Anglo-Indian relations."

At this, Nare-Jones bent forward, and in his turn examined the idol, while Savelsan smiled his thin, incredulous smile.

"These are ingenious theories," he said; "but we are really no nearer to facts, I am afraid."

"The only proof would be an inquiry into the former history of Medhans Lea; if events had happened there which would go to support this theory, why, then—But I cannot supply that information since I never heard of Medhans Lea or the ghost until I entered this room."

"I know something of Medhans Lea," put in Nare-Jones. "I found out a good deal about it before I left the place. And I must congratulate Mr. Low on his methods, for his theory tallies in a wonderful manner with the facts of the case. The house was long known to be haunted. It seems that many years ago a lady, the widow of an Indian officer, lived there with her only child, a boy, for whom she engaged a tutor, a dark-looking man, who wore a long black coat like a cassock, and was called 'the Jesuit' by the country people.

"One evening the man took the boy out into the shrubbery. Screams were heard, and when the child was brought in he was found to have lost his reason. He used to cry and shriek incessantly, but was never able to tell what had been done to him as long as he lived. As for this idol, the mother probably brought it with her from India, and the child used it as a toy, perhaps, because he was allowed no others."

"Yes," admitted Savelsan grudgingly. "But how about your sensations and Harland's seizure? You must know what was done to the child, Harland—what did you see in the shrubbery?"

Harland's florid face assumed a queer pallor.

"I saw something," replied he hesitatingly, "but I can't recall what it was. I only remember being possessed by a blind terror, and then nothing more until I recovered consciousness at the hotel next day."

"Can you account for this, Mr. Low?" asked Nare-Jones, "and there was also my strange notion of the whispering in the avenue."

"I think so," replied Flaxman Low. "I believe that the theory of atmospheric influences, which includes the power of environment to reproduce certain scenes and also thoughts, would throw light upon your sensations as well as Mr. Harland's. Such influences play a far larger part in our everyday experience than we have as yet any idea of."

There was a silence of a few moments; then Harland spoke—

"I fancy that we have said all that there is to be said upon the matter. We are much obliged to you, Mr. Low. I don't know how it strikes you other fellows, but, speaking for myself, I have seen enough of ghosts to last me for a very long time.

"And now," ended Harland wearily, "if you have no objection, we will pass on to pleasanter subjects."

THE STORY OF THE MOOR ROAD

"The medical profession must always have its own peculiar offshoots," said Mr. Flaxman Low, "some are trades, some mere hobbies, others, again, are allied subjects of a serious and profound nature. Now, as a student of psychical phenomena, I account myself only two degrees removed from the ordinary general practitioner."

"How do you make that out?" returned Colonel Daimley, pushing the decanter of old port invitingly across the table.

"The nerve and brain specialist is the link between myself and the man you would send for if you had a touch of lumbago," replied Low, with a slight smile. "Each division is but a higher grade of the same ladder—a step upwards into the unknown. I consider that I stand just one step above the specialist who makes a study of brain disease and insanity; he is at work on the disorders of the embodied spirit, while I deal with abnormal conditions of the free and detached spirit."

Colonel Daimley laughed aloud.

"That won't do, Low! No, no! First prove that your ghosts are sick."

"Certainly," replied Low gravely. "A very small proportion of spirits return as apparitions after the death of the body. Hence we may conclude that a ghost is a spirit in an abnormal condition. Abnormal conditions of the body usually indicate disease; why not of the spirit also?"

"That sounds fair enough," observed Lane Chaddam, the third man present. "Has the Colonel told you of our spook?"

The Colonel shook his handsome grey head in some irritation.

"You haven't convinced me yet, Lane, that it is a spook," he said dryly. "Human nature is at the bottom of most things in this world according to my opinion."

"What spook is this?" asked Flaxman Low. "I heard nothing of it when I was down with you last year."

"It's a recent acquisition," replied Lane Chaddam. "I wish we were rid of it, for my part."

"Have you seen it?" asked Low as he relit his long German pipe.

"Yes, and felt it!"

"What is it?"

"That's for you to say. He nearly broke my neck for me—that's all I can swear to."

Low knew Chaddam well. He was a long-limbed, athletic young fellow, with a good show of cups in his rooms, and was one of the various short-distance runners mentioned in the *Badminton* as having done the hundred in level time, and not the sort of man whose neck is easy to break.

"How did it happen?" asked Flaxman Low.

"About a fortnight ago," replied Chaddam, "I was flight-shooting near the burn where the hounds killed the otter last year. When the light began to fail, I thought I would come home by the old quarry, and pot anything that showed itself. As I walked along the far bank of the burn, I saw a man on the near side standing on the patch of sand below the reeds and watching me. As I came nearer I heard him coughing; it sounded like a sick cow. He stood still as if waiting for me. I thought it odd, because amongst the meres and water-meadows down there one never meets a stranger."

"Could you see him pretty clearly?"

"I saw his outline clearly, but not his face, because his back was toward the west. He was tall and jerry-built, so to speak, and had a little head no bigger than a child's, and he wore a fur cap with queer upstanding ears. When I came close, he suddenly slipped away; he jumped behind a big dyke, and I lost sight of him. But I didn't pay much attention; I had my gun, and I concluded it was a tramp."

"Tramps don't follow men of your size," observed Low, with a smile.

"This fellow did, at any rate. When I got across to the spot where he had been standing—the sand is soft there—I looked for his tracks. I knew he was bound to have a big foot of his own considering his height. But there were no footprints!"

"No footprints? You mean it was too dark for you to see them?" broke in Colonel Daimley.

"I am sure I should have seen them had there been any," persisted Chaddam quietly. "Besides, a man can't take a leap as he did without leaving a good hole behind him. The sand was perfectly smooth, because there had been a strong east wind all day. After looking about and seeing no marks, I went on to the top of the knoll above the quarry. After a bit I felt I was followed, though I couldn't see any one. You remember the thorn-bush that overhangs the quarry pool? I stopped there and bent over the edge of the cliff to see if there was anything in the pool. As I stooped I felt a point like a steel puncheon catch me in the small of the back. I kicked off from the quarry wall as well as I could, so as to avoid the broken rocks below, and I just managed to clear them, but I fell into the water with a flop that knocked the wind out of me. However, I held on to the gun, and, after a minute, I climbed to a ledge under the cliff and waited to see what my friend on top would do next. He waited too. I couldn't see him, but I heard him—he coughed up there in the dusk, the most ghastly noise I ever heard. The Colonel laughs at me, but it was about as nasty a half-hour as I care to have. In the end, I swam out across the pool and got home."

"I laugh at Lane," said the Colonel; "but all the same, it's a bad spot for a fall."

"You say he struck you in the back?" asked Flaxman Low, turning to Chaddam.

"Yes, and his finger was like a steel punch."

"What does Mrs. Daimley say to this affair?" went on Low presently.

"Not a word to my wife or Olivia, my dear Low!" exclaimed Colonel Daimley. "It would frighten them needlessly; besides, there would be an infernal fuss if we wanted to go flighting or anything after dark. I only fear for them, as they often drive into Nerbury by the Moor Road, which passes close by the quarry."

"Do they go in for their letters every evening as they used to do?"

"Just the same. And they won't take Stubbs with them, in spite of advice." The Colonel looked disconsolately at Low. "Women are angels, bless them! but they are the dickens to deal with, because they always want to know why."

"And now, Low, what have you to say about it?" asked Chaddam.

"Have you told me all?"

"Yes. The only other thing is that Livy says she hears some one coughing in the spinney most nights."

"'If all is as you say, Chaddam—pardon me, but in cases like this imagination is apt to play an unsuspected part—I should think that you have come upon a unique experience. What you have told me is not to be explained upon the lines of any ordinary theory."

After this they followed the ladies into the drawing-room, where they found Mrs. Daimley immersed in a novel as usual, and Livy looking pretty enough to account for the frequent presence of Lane Chaddam at Low Riddings. He was a distant cousin of the Colonel, and took advantage of his relationship to pay protracted visits to Northumberland.

Some years previous to the date of the above events, Colonel Daimley had bought and enlarged a substantial farmhouse which stood in a dip south of a lonely sweep of Northumbrian moors. It was a land of pale blue skies and far-off fringes of black and ragged pine-trees.

From the house a lane led over the windswept shoulder of the upland down to a hollow spanned by a railway bridge, then up again across the high levels of the moors until at length it lost itself in the outskirts of the little town of Nerbury. This Moor Road was peculiarly lonely; it approached but a single cottage the whole way, and ran very nearly over the door-step of that one—a deserted-looking slip of a place between the railway bridge and the quarry. Beyond the quarry stretched acres of marshland, meadows and reedy meres, all of which had been manipulated with such ability by the Colonel, that the duck-shooting on his land was the envy of the neighbourhood.

In spite of its loneliness the Moor Road was much frequented by the Daimleys, who preferred it to the high-road, which was uninteresting and much longer. Mrs. Daimley and Olivia drove in of an evening to fetch the letters—being people with nothing on earth to do, they were naturally always in a hurry to get their letters—and they perpetually had parcels waiting for them at the station which required to be called for at all sorts of hours. Thus it will be seen that the fact of the quarry being haunted by Lane Chaddam's assailant formed a very real danger to the inhabitants of Low Riddings.

At breakfast next day Livy said the tramp had been coughing in the spinney half the night.

"In what direction?" asked Flaxman Low.

Livy pointed to the window which looked on to the gate and the thick boundary hedge, the last still full of crisp ruddy leaves.

"You feel an interest in your tramp, Miss Daimley?"

"Of course, poor creature! I wanted to go out to look for him the other night, but they would not allow me."

"That was before we knew he was so interesting," said Chaddam. "I promise we'll catch him for you next time he comes."

And this was in fact the programme they tried to carry out, but although the coughing was heard in the spinney, no one even caught a glimpse of any living thing moving or hiding among the trees.

The next stage of the affair happened to be an experience of Livy. In some excitement she told the assembled family at dinner that she had just seen the coughing tramp.

Lane Chaddam changed colour.

"You don't mean to say, Livy, that you went to search for him alone?" he exclaimed half-angrily.

Flaxman Low and the Colonel wisely went on eating oyster patties without taking any apparent notice of the girl's news.

"Why shouldn't I?" asked Livy quickly, "but as it happens, I saw him in Scully's cottage by the quarry this evening."

"What?" exclaimed Colonel Daimley, "in Scully's cottage. I'll see to that."

"Why? Are you all so prejudiced against my poor tramp?"

"On the contrary," replied Flaxman Low, "we all want to know what he's like."

"So odd-looking! I was driving home alone from the post when, as I passed the quarry cottage, I heard the cough. You know it is quite unmistakable; I looked up at the window, and there he was. I have never seen anybody in the least like him. His face is ghastly pale and perfectly hairless, and he has such a little head. He stared at me so threateningly that I whipped up Lorelie."

"Were you frightened, then?"

"Not exactly, but he had such a wicked face that I drove away as fast as I could."

"I understood that you had arranged to send Stubbs for the letters?" said Colonel Daimley, with some annoyance. "Why can't girls say what they mean?"

Livy made no reply, and after a pause Chaddam put a question.

"You must have passed along the Moor Road about seven o'clock?"

"Yes, it was after six when I left the Post Office," replied Livy. "Why?"

"It was quite dark—how did you see the hairless man so plainly? I was round on the marshes all the evening, and I am quite certain there was no light at any time in Scully's cottage."

"I don't remember whether there was any light behind him in the room," returned Livy, after a moment's consideration; "I only know that I saw his head and face quite plainly."

There was no more said on the subject at the time, though the Colonel forbade Livy to run any further risks by going alone on the Moor Road. After this the three men paraded the lane and lay in wait for the hairless tramp or ghost. On the second evening their watch was rewarded, when Chaddam came hurriedly into the smoking-room to say that the coughing could at that instant be heard in the hedge by the dining-room. It was still early, although the evening had closed in with clouds, and all outside was dark. “I’ll deal with him this time effectually!” exclaimed the Colonel. “I’ll slip out the back way, and lie in the hedge down the road by the field gate. You two must chivy him out to me, and when he comes along, I’ll have him against the sky-line and give him a charge of № 4 if he shows fight.”

The Colonel stole down the lane while the others beat the spinney and hedge, Flaxman Low very much chagrined at being forced to deal with an interesting problem in this rough and ready fashion. However, he saw that on this occasion at least it would be useless to oppose the Colonel’s notions. When he and Chaddam met after beating the hedge they saw a tall figure shamble away rapidly down the lane towards the Colonel’s hiding-place.

They stood still and waited for developments, but the minutes followed each other in intense stillness. Then they went to find the Colonel.

“Hullo, Colonel, anything wrong?” asked Chaddam, on nearing the field gate.

The Colonel straightened himself with the help of Chaddam’s arm.

“Did you see him?” he whispered.

“We thought so. Why did you not fire?”

“Because,” said the Colonel in a husky voice, “I had no gun!”

“But you took it with you?”

“Yes.”

Flaxman Low opened the lantern he carried, and, as the light swept round in a wide circle, something glinted on the grass. It was the stock of the Colonel’s gun. A little further off they came upon the Damascus barrels bent and twisted into a ball like so much fine wire. Presently the Colonel explained.

"I saw him coming and meant to meet him, but I seemed dazed—I couldn't move! The gun was snatched from me, and I made no resistance—I don't know why." He took the gun-barrels and examined them slowly. "I give in, Low; no human hand did that."

During dinner Flaxman Low said abruptly: "I suspect you have lately had an earthquake down here."

"How did you know?" asked Livy. "Have you been to the quarry?"

Low said he had not.

"It was such a poor little earthquake that even the papers did not think it worth while to mention it!" went on Livy. "We didn't feel any shock, and, in fact, knew nothing about it, until Dr. Petterped told us."

"You had a landslip though?" went on Low.

Livy opened her pretty eyes.

"But you know all about it," she said. "Yes, the landslip was just by the old quarry."

"I should like to see the place to-morrow," observed Low.

Next day, therefore, when the Colonel went off to the coverts with a couple of neighbours, whom he had invited to join him, Flaxman Low accompanied Chaddam to examine the scene of the landslip.

From the edge of the upland, looking across the hollow crowded with reedy pools, they could see in the torn, reddish flank of the opposite slope the sharp tilt of the broken strata. To the right of this lay the old quarry, and about a hundred yards to the left the lonely house and the curving road.

Low descended into the hollow and spent a long time in the spongy ground between the back of the quarry and the lower edge of the newly uncovered strata, using his little hammer freely, especially about one narrow black fissure round which he sniffed and pottered in absorbed silence. Presently he called to Chaddam.

"There has been a slight explosion of gas—a rare gas, here," he said. "I hardly hoped to find traces of it, but it is unmistakable."

"Very unmistakable," agreed Chaddam, with a laugh. "You'd have said so had you been here when it happened."

"Ah, very satisfactory indeed. And that was a fortnight ago, you say?"

"Rather more now. It took place a couple of days before my fall into the quarry pool."

"Any one ill near by—at that cottage, for instance?" asked Low, as he joined Chaddam.

"Why? Was that gas poisonous? There's a man in the Colonel's employ named Scully in that cottage, who has had pneumonia, but he was on the mend when the land-slip occurred. Since then he has grown steadily worse."

"Is there any one with him?"

"Yes, the Daimleys sent for a woman to look after him. Scully's a very decent man. I often go in to see him."

"And so does the hairless man, apparently," added Low.

"No; that's the queer part of it. Neither he nor the woman in charge have ever seen such a person as Livy described. I don't know what to think."

"The first thing to be done is to get the man from here at once," said Low decidedly. "Let's go in and see him."

They found Scully low and drowsy. The nurse shook her head at the two visitors in a despondent way.

"He grows weaker day by day," she said.

"Get him away from here at once," repeated Low, as they went out.

"We might have him up at Low Riddings, but he seems almost too weak to be moved," replied Chaddam doubtfully.

"My dear fellow, it's his only chance of life."

The Daimleys made arrangements for the reception of Scully, provided Dr. Thomson of Nerbury gave his consent to the removal. In the afternoon, therefore, Chaddam bicycled into Nerbury to see the doctor on the subject.

"If I were you, Chaddam," said Low, before he started, "I'd be back by daylight."

Unfortunately Dr. Thomson was on his rounds, and did not return until after dark, by which time it was too late to remove Scully that evening. After leaving the doctor's house Chaddam went to the station to inquire about a box from Mudie's. The books having arrived, he took out a couple of volumes for Mrs. Daimley's present consumption, and was strapping them on in front of his bicycle, when it struck him that unless he went home by the Moor Road he would be late for dinner.

Accordingly he branched off into the bare track which led over the moors. The twilight had deepened into a fine, cold night, and a moon was swinging up into a pale, clear sky. The spread of heather, purple in the daytime, appeared jet black by moonlight, and across it he could see the white ribbon of road stretching ahead into the distance. The scents of the night were fresh in his nostrils, as he ran easily along the level with the breeze behind him.

He soon reached the incline past Scully's cottage. Well away to the left lay the quarry pool like a blotch of ink under its shadowing cliff. There was no light in the cottage, and it seemed even more deserted-looking than usual.

As Chaddam flashed under the bridge, he heard a cough, and glanced back over his shoulder. A tall, loose-jointed form he had seen once before was rearing itself up upon the railway bridge. There was something curiously un-human about the lank outlines and the cant of the small head with its prick-eared cap showing out so clearly against the lighter sky behind.

When Chaddam looked again, he saw the thing on the bridge fling up its long arms and leap down on to the road some thirty feet below.

Then Chaddam rode. He began to think he had been a fool to come, and he counted that he was a good mile from home. At first he fancied he heard footfalls, then he fancied there were none. The hard road flew under him, all thoughts of economising his strength were lost, his single aim was to make the pace.

Suddenly his bicycle jerked violently, and he was shot over into the road. As he fell, he turned his head and was conscious of a little, bleached, bestial face, wet with fury, not ten yards behind!

He sprang to his feet, and ran up the road as he had never run before. He ran wonderfully, but he might as well have tried to race a cheetah. It was not a question of speed, the game was in the hands of this thing with the limbs of a starved Hercules, whose bony knees seemed to leap into its ghastly face at every stride. Chaddam topped the slope with a sickening sense of his own powerlessness. Already he saw Low Riddings in the distance, and a dim light came creeping along the road towards him. Another frantic spurt, and he had almost reached the light, when a hand closed like a vice on his shoulder, and seemed to fasten on the flesh. He rushed blindly on towards the house. He saw the door-handle gleam, and in another second he had pitched head foremost on to the knotted matting in the hall.

When he recovered his senses his first question was: "Where is Low?"

"Didn't you meet him?" asked Livy, "I—that is, we were anxious about you, as you were so late, and I was just starting to meet you when Mr. Low came downstairs and insisted on going instead."

Chaddam stood up.

"I must follow him."

But as he spoke the front door opened, and Flaxman Low entered, and looked up at the clock.

"Eight-fifteen," he said. "You're late, Chaddam."

Afterwards, in the smoking-room, he gave an account of what he had seen.

"I saw Chaddam racing up the road with a tall figure behind him. It stretched out its hand and grasped his shoulder. The next instant it stopped short as if it had been shot. It seemed to reel back and collapse, and then limped off into the hedge like a disappointed dog."

Chaddam stood up and began to take off his coat.

"Whatever the thing is, it is something out of the common. Look here!" he said, turning up his shirt sleeve over the point of his shoulder, where three singular marks were visible, irregularly placed as the fingers of a hand might fall. They were oblong in shape, about the size of a bean, and swollen in purple lumps well above the surface of the skin.

"Looks as if some one had been using a small cupping-glass on you," remarked the Colonel uneasily. "What do you say to it, Low?"

"I say that since Chaddam has escaped with his life, I have only to congratulate him on what, in Europe certainly, is a unique adventure."

The Colonel threw his cigar into the fire.

"Such adventures are too dangerous for my taste," he said. "This creature has on two occasions murderously attacked Lane Chaddam, and it would, no doubt, have attacked Livy if it had had the chance. We must leave this place at once, or we shall be murdered in our beds!"

"I don't think, Colonel, that you will be troubled with this mysterious visitant again," replied Flaxman Low.

"Why not? Who or what is this horrible thing?"

"I believe it to be an Elemental Earth Spirit," returned Low. "No other solution fits the facts of the case."

"What is an Elemental?" resumed the Colonel irritably. "Remember, Low, I expect you to prove your theories so that a plain man may understand, if I am to stay on at Low Riddings."

"Eastern occultists describe wandering tribes of earth spirits, evil intelligences, possessing spirit as distinct from soul—all inimical to man."

"But how do you know that the thing on the Moor Road is an Elemental?"

"Because the points of resemblance are curiously remarkable. The occultists say that when these spirits materialise, they appear in grotesque and uncouth forms; secondly, that they are invariably bloodless and hairless; thirdly, they move with extraordinary rapidity, and leave no footprints; and lastly, their agility and strength is superhuman. All these peculiarities have been observed in connection with the figure on the Moor Road."

"I admit that no man I have ever met with," commented Colonel Daimley, "could jump uninjured from a height of thirty feet, race a bicycle, and twist up gun-barrels like so much soft paper. So perhaps you're right. But can you tell me why or how it came here?"

"My conclusions," began Low, "may seem to you far-fetched and ridiculous, but you must give them the benefit of the fact that they precisely account for the otherwise unaccountable features which mark this affair. I connect this appearance with the earthquake and the sick man."

"What? Scully in league with the devil?" exclaimed the Colonel bluntly. "Why, the man is too weak to leave his bed; besides, he is a short, thick-set fellow, entirely unlike our haunting friend."

"You mistake me, Colonel," said Low, in his quiet tones. "These Elementals cannot take visible form without drawing upon the resources of the living. They absorb the vitality of any ailing person until it is exhausted, and the person dies."

"Then they begin operations upon a fresh victim? A pleasant look-out to know we keep a well-attested vampire in the neighbourhood!"

"Vampires are a distinct race, with different methods; one being that the Elemental is a wanderer, and goes far afield to search for a new victim."

"But why should it want to kill me?" put in Chaddam.

"As I have told you, they are animated solely by a blind malignity to the human race, and you happened to be handy."

"But the earthquake, Low; where is the connection there?" demanded the Colonel, with the air of a man who intends to corner his opponent.

Flaxman Low lit one cigar at the end of another before he replied.

"At this point," he said, "my own theories and observations and those of the old occultists overlap. The occultists held that some of these spirits are imprisoned in the interior of the earth, but may be set free in consequence of those shiftings and disturbances which take place during an earthquake. This in more modern language simply means that Elementals are in some manner connected with certain of the primary strata. Now, my own researches have led me to conclude that atmospheric influences are intimately associated with spiritual phenomena. Some gases appear to be productive of such phenomena. One of these is generated when certain of the primary formations are newly exposed to the common air."

"This is almost beyond belief—I don't understand you," said the Colonel.

"I am sorry that I cannot give you all the links in my own chain of reasoning," returned Low. "Much is still obscure, but the evidence is sufficiently strong to convince me that in such a case of earthquake and landslip as has lately taken place here the phenomenon of an embodied Elemental might possibly be expected to follow, given the one necessary adjunct of a sick person in the near neighbourhood of the disturbance."

"But when this brute got hold of me, why didn't it finish me off?" asked Chaddam. "Or was it your coming that prevented it?"

Flaxman Low considered.

"No; I don't think I can flatter myself that my coming had anything to do with your escape. It was a near thing—how near you will understand when we hear further news of Scully in the morning."

A servant entered the room at this moment.

"The woman has come up from the cottage, sir, to say that Scully is dead."

"At what hour did he die?" asked Low.

"About ten minutes past eight, sir, she says."

"Five minutes before I got in. The hour agrees exactly," commented Low, when the man had left the room. "The figure stopped and collapsed so suddenly that I believed something of this kind must have happened."

"But surely this is a very unprecedented occurrence?"

"It is," said Flaxman Low. "But I can assure you that if you take the trouble to glance through the pages of the psychical periodicals you will find many statements at least as wonderful."

"But are they true?"

Flaxman Low shrugged his shoulders.

"At any rate," said he, "we know this is."

The Daimleys have spent many pleasant days at Low Riddings since then, but Chaddam—who has acquired a right to control Miss Livy's actions more or less—persists in his objection to any solitary expeditions to Nerbury along the Moor Road. For, although the figure has never been seen about Low Riddings since, some strange stories have lately appeared in the papers of a similar mysterious figure which has been met with more than once in the lonelier spots about North London. If it be true that this nameless wandering spirit, with the strength and activity of twenty men, still haunts our lonely roads, the sooner Mr. Flaxman Low exorcises it the better.

THE STORY OF BAELBROW

It is a matter for regret that so many of Mr. Flaxman Low's reminiscences should deal with the darker episodes of his career. Yet this is almost unavoidable, as the more purely scientific and less strongly marked cases would not, perhaps, contain the same elements of interest for the general public, however valuable and instructive they might be to the expert student. It has also been considered better to choose the completer cases, those that ended in something like satisfactory proof, rather than the many instances where the thread broke off abruptly amongst surmisings, which it was never possible to subject to convincing tests.

North of a low-lying strip of country on the East Anglian coast, the promontory of Bael Ness thrusts out a blunt nose into the sea. On the Ness, backed by pinewoods, stands a square, comfortable stone mansion, known to the countryside as Baelbrow. It has faced the east winds for close upon three hundred years, and during the whole period has been the home of the Swaffam family, who were never in anywise put out of conceit of their ancestral dwelling by the fact that it had always been haunted. Indeed the Swaffams were proud of the Baelbrow Ghost, which enjoyed a wide notoriety, and no one dreamt of complaining of its behaviour until Professor Jungvort, of Nuremberg, laid information against it, and sent an urgent appeal for help to Mr. Flaxman Low.

The Professor, who was well acquainted with Mr. Low, detailed the circumstances of his tenancy of Baelbrow, and the unpleasant events that had followed thereupon.

It appeared that Mr. Swaffam, senior, who spent a large portion of his time abroad, had offered to lend his house to the Professor for the summer season. When the Jungvorts arrived at Baelbrow, they were charmed with the place. The prospect, though not very varied, was at least extensive, and the air exhilarating. Also the Professor's daughter enjoyed frequent visits from her betrothed—Harold Swaffam—and the Professor was delightfully employed in overhauling the Swaffam library.

The Jungvorts had been duly told of the ghost, which lent distinction to the old house, but never in any way interfered with the comfort of its inmates. For some time they found this description to be strictly true, but with the beginning of October came a change. Up to this time, and as far back as the Swaffam annals reached, the ghost had been a shadow, a rustle, a passing sigh—nothing definite or troublesome. But early in October strange things began to occur, and the terror culminated when a housemaid was found dead in a corridor three weeks later. Upon this the Professor felt that it was time to send for Flaxman Low.

Mr. Low arrived upon a chilly evening, when the house was already beginning to blur in the purple twilight, and the resinous scent of the pines came sweetly on the land breeze. Jungvort welcomed him in the spacious, fire-lit hall. He was a stout German with a quantity of white hair, round eyes emphasised by spectacles, and a kindly, dreamy face. His life-study was philology, and his two relaxations chess and the smoking of a big Bismarck-bowled meerschaum.

"Now, Professor," said Mr. Low, when they had settled themselves in the smoking-room, "how did it all begin?"

"I will tell you," replied Jungvort, thrusting out his chin and tapping his broad chest, and speaking as if an unwarrantable liberty had been taken with him. "First of all, it has shown itself to me!"

Mr. Flaxman Low smiled, and assured him that nothing could be more satisfactory.

"But not at all satisfactory!" exclaimed the Professor. "I was sitting here alone, it might have been midnight—when I hear something come creeping like a little dog with its nails, tick-tick, upon the oak flooring of the hall. I whistle, for I think it is the little 'Rags' of my daughter, and afterwards opened the door, and I saw"—he hesitated, and looked hard at Low through his spectacles—"something that was just disappearing into the passage which connects the two wings of the house. It was a figure, not unlike the human figure, but narrow and straight. I fancied I saw a bunch of black hair, and a flutter of something detached, which may have been a handkerchief. I was overcome by a feeling of repulsion. I heard a few clicking steps, which stopped, as I thought, at the museum door. Come, I will show you the spot."

The Professor conducted Mr. Low into the hall. The main staircase, dark and massive, yawned above them, and directly behind it ran the passage referred to by the

Professor. It was over twenty feet long, and about midway led past a deep arch containing a door reached by two steps. Jungvort explained that this door formed the entrance to a large room called the museum, in which Mr. Swaffam, senior, who was something of a dilettante, stored the various curios he picked up during his excursions abroad. The Professor went on to say that he immediately followed the figure, which he believed had gone into the museum, but he found nothing there except the cases containing Swaffam's treasures.

"I mentioned my experience to no one. I concluded that I had seen the ghost. But two days after, one of the female servants, coming through the passage in the dark, declared that a man leapt out at her from the embrasure of the museum door, but she released herself and ran screaming into the servants' hall. We at once made a search, but found nothing to substantiate her story.

"I took no notice of this, though it coincided pretty well with my own experience. The week after, my daughter Lena came down late one night for a book. As she was about to cross the hall, something leapt upon her from behind. Women are of little use in serious investigations—she fainted! Since then she has been ill, and the doctor says 'run down.'" Here the Professor spread out his hands. "So she leaves for a change to-morrow. Since then other members of the household have been attacked in much the same manner, with always the same result—they faint, and are weak and useless when they recover.

"But, last Wednesday, the affair became a tragedy. By that time the servants had refused to come through the passage except in a crowd of three or four—most of them preferring to go round by the terrace to reach this part of the house. But one maid, named Eliza Freeman, said she was not afraid of the Baelbrow Ghost, and undertook to put out the lights in the hall one night. When she had done so, and was returning through the passage past the museum door, she appears to have been attacked, or at any rate frightened. In the grey of the morning they found her lying beside the steps dead. There was a little blood upon her sleeve, but no mark upon her body except a small raised pustule under the ear. The doctor said the girl was extraordinarily anæmic, and that she probably died from fright, her heart being weak. I was surprised at this, for she had always seemed to be a particularly strong and active young woman."

"Can I see Miss Jungvort to-morrow before she goes?" asked Low, as the Professor signified he had nothing more to tell.

The Professor was rather unwilling that his daughter should be questioned, but at last gave his permission, and next morning Low had a short talk with the girl before she left the house. He found her a very pretty girl, though listless and startlingly pale, and with a frightened stare in her light brown eyes. Mr. Low asked if she could describe her assailant.

"No," she answered, "I could not see him, for he was behind me. I only saw a dark, bony hand, with shining nails, and a bandaged arm pass just under my eyes before I fainted."

"Bandaged arm? I have heard nothing of this."

"Tut—tut, mere fancy!" put in the Professor impatiently.

"I saw the bandages on the arm," repeated the girl, turning her head wearily away, "and I smelt the antiseptics it was dressed with."

"You have hurt your neck," remarked Mr. Low, who noticed a small circular patch of pink under her ear.

She flushed and paled, raising her hand to her neck with a nervous jerk, as she said in a low voice—

"It has almost killed me. Before he touched me, I knew he was there! I felt it!"

When they left her the Professor apologised for the unreliability of her evidence, and pointed out the discrepancy between her statement and his own.

"She says she sees nothing but an arm, yet I tell you it had no arms! Preposterous! Conceive a wounded man entering this house to frighten the young women! I do not know what to make of it! Is it a man, or is it the Baelbrow Ghost?"

During the afternoon, when Mr. Low and the Professor returned from a stroll on the shore, they found a dark-browed young man, with a bull-neck and strongly marked features, standing sullenly before the hall fire. The Professor presented him to Mr. Low as Harold Swaffam.

Swaffam seemed to be about thirty, but was already known as a far-seeing and successful member of the Stock Exchange.

"I am pleased to meet you, Mr. Low," he began, with a keen glance, "though you don't look sufficiently high-strung for one of your profession."

Mr. Low merely bowed.

"Come, you don't defend your craft against my insinuations?" went on Swaffam. "And so you are here to rout out our poor old ghost from Baelbrow? You forget that he is an heirloom, a family possession! What's this about his having turned rabid, eh, Professor?" he ended, wheeling round upon Jungvort in his brusque way.

The Professor told the story over again. It was plain that he stood rather in awe of his prospective son-in-law.

"I heard much the same from Lena, whom I met at the station," said Swaffam. "It is my opinion that the women in this house are suffering from an epidemic of hysteria. You agree with me, Mr. Low?"

"Possibly. Though hysteria could hardly account for Freeman's death."

"I can't say as to that until I have looked further into the particulars. I have not been idle since I arrived. I have examined the museum. No one has entered it from the outside, and there is no other way of entrance except through the passage. The flooring is laid, I happen to know, on a thick layer of concrete. And there the case for the ghost stands at present." After a few moments of dogged reflection, he swung round on Mr. Low, in a manner that seemed peculiar to him when about to address any person. "What do you say to this plan, Mr. Low? I propose to drive the Professor over to Ferryvale, to stop there for a day or two at the hotel, and I will also dispose of the servants who still remain in the house for, say, forty-eight hours. Meanwhile you and I can try to go further into the secret of the ghost's new pranks?"

Flaxman Low replied that this scheme exactly met his views, but the Professor protested against being sent away. Harold Swaffam, however, was a man who liked to arrange things in his own fashion, and within forty-five minutes he and Jungvort departed in the dogcart.

The evening was lowering, and Baelbrow, like all houses built in exposed situations, was extremely susceptible to the changes of the weather. Therefore, before many hours were over, the place was full of creaking noises as the screaming gale battered at the shuttered windows, and the tree-branches tapped and groaned against the walls.

Harold Swaffam, on his way back, was caught in the storm and drenched to the skin. It was therefore settled that after he had changed his clothes he should have a couple of hours' rest on the smoking-room sofa, while Mr. Low kept watch in the hall.

The early part of the night passed over uneventfully. A light burned faintly in the great wainscoted hall, but the passage was dark. There was nothing to be heard but the wild moan and whistle of the wind coming in from the sea, and the squalls of rain dashing against the windows. As the hours advanced, Mr. Low lit a lantern that lay at hand, and, carrying it along the passage, tried the museum door. It yielded, and the wind came muttering through to meet him. He looked round at the shutters, and behind the big cases which held Mr. Swaffam's treasures, to make sure that the room contained no living occupant but himself.

Suddenly, he fancied he heard a scraping noise behind him, and turned round, but discovered nothing to account for it. Finally, he laid the lantern on a bench so that its light should fall through the door into the passage, and returned again to the hall, where he put out the lamp, and then once more took up his station by the closed door of the smoking-room.

A long hour passed, during which the wind continued to roar down the wide hall chimney, and the old boards creaked as if furtive footsteps were gathering from every corner of the house. But Flaxman Low heeded none of these things; he was waiting for a certain sound.

After a while, he heard it—the cautious scraping of wood on wood. He leant forward to watch the museum door. Click, click, came the curious dog-like tread upon the tiled floor of the museum, till the thing, whatever it was, paused and listened behind the open door. The wind lulled at the moment, and Low listened also, but no further sound was to be heard, only slowly across the broad ray of light falling through the door grew a stealthy shadow.

Again the wind rose, and blew in heavy gusts about the house, till even the flame in the lantern flickered; but when it steadied once more, Flaxman Low saw that the silent form had passed through the door, and was now on the steps outside. He could just make out a dim shadow in the dark angle of the embrasure.

Presently, from the shapeless shadow came a sound Mr. Low was not prepared to hear. The thing sniffed the air with the strong, audible inspiration of a bear, or some large animal. At the same moment, carried on the draughts of the hall, a faint, unfamiliar odour reached his nostrils. Lena Jungvort's words flashed back upon him: this, then, was the creature with the bandaged arm!

Again, as the storm shrieked and shook the windows, a darkness passed across the light. The thing had sprung out from the angle of the door, and Flaxman Low knew that it was making its way towards him through the illusive blackness of the hall. He hesitated for a second; then he opened the smoking-room door.

Harold Swaffam sat up on the sofa, dazed with sleep.

"What has happened? Has it come?"

Low told him what he had just seen. Swaffam listened half-smilingly.

"What do you make of it now?" he said.

"I must ask you to defer that question for a little," replied Low.

"Then you mean me to suppose that you have a theory to fit all these incongruous items?"

"I have a theory which may be modified by further knowledge," said Low. "Meantime, am I right in concluding from the name of this house that it was built on a barrow or burying-place?"

"You are right, though that has nothing to do with the latest freaks of our ghost," returned Swaffam decidedly.

"I also gather that Mr. Swaffam has lately sent home one of the many cases now lying in the museum?" went on Mr. Low.

"He sent one, certainly, last September."

"And you have opened it," asserted Low.

"Yes; though I flattered myself I had left no trace of my handiwork."

"I have not examined the cases," said Low. "I inferred that you had done so from other facts."

"Now, one thing more," went on Swaffam, still smiling. "Do you imagine there is any danger—I mean to men like ourselves? Hysterical women cannot be taken into serious account."

"Certainly; the gravest danger to any person who moves about this part of the house alone after dark," replied Low.

Harold Swaffam leant back and crossed his legs.

"To go back to the beginning of our conversation, Mr. Low, may I remind you of the various conflicting particulars you will have to reconcile before you can present any decent theory to the world?"

"I am quite aware of that."

"First of all, our original ghost was a mere misty presence, rather guessed at from vague sounds and shadows—now we have a something that is tangible, and that can, as we have proof, kill with fright. Next, Jungvort declares the thing was a narrow, long, and distinctly armless object, while Miss Jungvort has not only seen the arm and hand of a human being, but saw them clearly enough to tell us that the nails were gleaming and the arm bandaged. She also felt its strength. Jungvort, on the other hand, maintained that it clicked along like a dog—you bear out this description with the additional information that it sniffs like a wild beast. Now, what can this thing be? It is capable of being seen, smelt, and felt, yet it hides itself successfully in a room where there is no cavity or space sufficient to afford covert to a cat! You still tell me that you believe that you can explain?"

"Most certainly," replied Flaxman Low with conviction.

"I have not the slightest intention or desire to be rude, but as a mere matter of common sense, I must express my opinion plainly. I believe the whole thing to be the result of excited imaginations, and I am about to prove it. Do you think there is any further danger to-night?"

"Very great danger to-night," replied Low.

"Very well; as I said, I am going to prove it. I will ask you to allow me to lock you up in one of the distant rooms, where I can get no help from you, and I will pass the remainder of the night walking about the passage and hall in the dark. That should give proof one way or the other."

"You can do so if you wish; but I must at least beg to be allowed to look on. I will leave the house, and watch what happens from the window in the passage, which I saw opposite the museum door. You cannot, in any fairness, refuse to let me be a witness."

"I cannot, of course," returned Swaffam. "Still, the night is too bad to turn a dog out into, and I warn you that I shall lock you out."

"That will not matter. Lend me a macintosh, and leave the lantern lit in the museum where I placed it."

Swaffam agreed to this. Mr. Low gives a graphic account of what followed. He left the house, and was duly locked out, and, after groping his way round by the walls, found himself at length outside the window of the passage, which was almost opposite to the door of the museum. The door was still ajar, and a thin band of light cut out into the gloom. Further down, the hall gaped black and void. Low, sheltering himself as well as he could from the rain, waited for Swaffam's appearance. Was the terrible yellow watcher balancing itself upon its lean legs in the dim corner opposite, ready to spring out with its deadly strength upon the passer-by?

Presently Low heard a door bang inside the house, and the next moment Swaffam appeared with a candle in his hand, an isolated spread of weak rays against the vast darkness behind. He advanced steadily down the passage, his dark face grim and set, and as he came Mr. Low experienced that tingling sensation which is so often the forerunner of some strange experience. Swaffam passed on towards the other end of the passage. There was a quick vibration of the museum door as a lean shape with a shrunken head leapt out into the passage after him. Then all together came a hoarse shout, the noise of a fall, and utter darkness.

In an instant Mr. Low had broken the glass, opened the window, and swung himself into the passage. There he lit a match, and as it flared he saw by its dim light a picture painted for a second upon the obscurity beyond.

Swaffam's big figure lay with outstretched arms, face downwards, and as Low looked a crouching shape extricated itself from the fallen man, raising a narrow, vicious head from his shoulder.

The match spluttered feebly and went out, and Low heard a flying step click on the boards, before he could find the candle Swaffam had dropped. Lighting it, he stooped over Swaffam and turned him on his back. The man's strong colour had gone, and the wax-white face looked whiter still against the blackness of hair and brows, and upon his neck, under the ear, was a little raised pustule, from which a thin line of blood was streaked up to the angle of his cheekbone.

Some instinctive feeling prompted Low to glance up at this moment. Half extended from the museum doorway were a face and bony neck—a high-nosed, dull-eyed, malignant face, the eye-sockets hollow, and the darkened teeth showing. Low plunged his hand into his pocket, and a shot rang out in the echoing passage-way and hall. The wind sighed through the broken panes, a ribbon of stuff fluttered along the polished flooring, and that was all, as Flaxman Low half dragged, half carried Swaffam into the smoking-room.

It was some time before Swaffam recovered consciousness. He listened to Low's story of how he had found him with an angry gleam in his sombre eyes.

"The ghost has scored off me," he said, with an odd, sullen laugh, "but now I fancy it's my turn! But before we adjourn to the museum to examine the place, I will ask you to let me hear your notion of things. You have been right in saying there was real danger. For myself I can only tell you that I felt something spring upon me, and I knew no more. Had this not happened I am afraid I should never have asked you a second time what your idea of the matter might be," he ended, with a sort of sulky frankness.

"There are two main indications," replied Low. "This strip of yellow bandage, which I have just now picked up from the passage floor, and the mark on your neck."

"What's that you say?" Swaffam rose quickly and examined his neck in a small glass beside the mantel-shelf.

"Connect those two, and I think I can leave you to work it out for yourself," said Low.

"Pray let us have your theory in full," requested Swaffam shortly.

"Very well," answered Low good-humouredly—he thought Swaffam's annoyance natural under the circumstances. "The long, narrow figure which seemed to the Professor to be armless is developed on the next occasion. For Miss Jungvort sees a bandaged arm and a dark hand with gleaming—which means, of course, gilded—nails. The clicking sound of the footstep coincides with these particulars, for we know that sandals made of strips of leather are not uncommon in company with gilt finger-nails and bandages. Old and dry leather would naturally click upon your polished floors."

"Bravo, Mr. Low! So you mean to say that this house is haunted by a mummy!"

"That is my idea, and all I have seen confirms me in my opinion."

"To do you justice, you held this theory before to-night—before, in fact, you had seen anything for yourself. You gathered that my father had sent home a mummy, and you went on to conclude that I had opened the case?"

"Yes. I imagine you took off most of, or rather all, the outer bandages, thus leaving the limbs free, wrapped only in the inner bandages which were swathed round each separate limb. I fancy this mummy was preserved on the Theban method, with aromatic spices, which left the skin olive-coloured, dry and flexible, like tanned leather, the features remaining distinct, and the hair, teeth, and eyebrows perfect."

"So far good," said Swaffam. "But now, how about the intermittent vitality? The pustule on the neck of those whom it attacks? And where is our old Baelbrow ghost to come in?"

Swaffam tried to speak in a rallying tone, but his excitement and lowering temper were visible enough, in spite of the attempts he made to suppress them.

"To begin at the beginning," said Flaxman Low, "everybody who, in a rational and honest manner, investigates the phenomena of spiritism will, sooner or later, meet in them some perplexing element, which is not to be explained by any of the ordinary theories. For reasons into which I need not now enter, this present case appears to me to be one of these. I am led to believe that the ghost which has for so many years given dim and vague manifestations of its existence in this house is a vampire."

Swaffam threw back his head with an incredulous gesture.

"We no longer live in the middle ages, Mr. Low! And besides, how could a vampire come here?" he said scoffingly.

"It is held by some authorities on these subjects that under certain conditions a vampire may be self-created. You tell me that this house is built upon an ancient barrow—in fact, on a spot where we might naturally expect to find such an elemental psychic germ. In those dead human systems were contained all the seeds for good and evil. The power which causes these psychic seeds or germs to grow is thought, and from being long dwelt on and indulged, a thought might finally gain a mysterious vitality, which could go on increasing more and more by attracting to itself suitable and appropriate elements from its environment. For a long period this germ remained a helpless intelligence, awaiting the opportunity to assume some material form, by means of which to carry out its desires. The invisible is the real; the material only subserves its manifestation. The impalpable reality already existed, when you provided for it a physical medium for action by unwrapping the mummy's form. Now, we can only judge of the nature of the germ by its manifestation through matter. Here we have every indication of a vampire intelligence touching into life and energy the dead human frame. Hence the mark on the neck of its victims, and their bloodless and anæmic condition. For a vampire, as you know, sucks blood."

Swaffam rose, and took up the lamp.

"Now, for proof," he said bluntly. "Wait a second, Mr. Low. You say you fired at this appearance?" And he took up the pistol which Low had laid down on the table.

"Yes, I aimed at a small portion of its foot which I saw on the step."

Without more words, and with the pistol still in his hand, Swaffam led the way to the museum.

The wind howled round the house, and the darkness which precedes the dawn lay upon the world, when the two men looked upon one of the strangest sights it has ever been given to men to shudder at.

Half in and half out of an oblong wooden box in a corner of the great room lay a lean shape in its rotten yellow bandages, the scraggy neck surmounted by a mop of frizzled hair. The toe-strap of a sandal and a portion of the right foot had been shot away.

Swaffam, with a working face, gazed down at it, then seizing it by its tearing bandages, he flung it into the box, where it fell into a life-like posture, its wide, moist-lipped mouth gaping up at them.

For a moment Swaffam stood over the thing; then with a curse he raised the revolver and shot into the grinning face again and again with a deliberate vindictiveness. Finally he rammed the thing down into the box, and, clubbing the weapon, smashed the head into fragments with a vicious energy that coloured the whole horrible scene with a suggestion of murder done.

Then, turning to Low, he said—

"Help me to fasten the cover on it."

"Are you going to bury it?"

"No, we must rid the earth of it," he answered savagely. "I'll put it into the old canoe and burn it."

The rain had ceased, when in the daybreak they carried the old canoe down to the shore. In it they placed the mummy case with its ghastly occupant, and piled fagots about it. The sail was raised and the pile lighted, and Low and Swaffam watched it creep out on the ebb-tide, at first a twinkling spark, then a flare of waving fire, until far out to sea the history of that dead thing ended three thousand years after the priests of Amen had laid it to rest in its appointed pyramid.

THE STORY OF THE GREY HOUSE

Mr. Flaxman Low declares that only on one occasion has he undertaken, unasked, the solving of a psychical mystery. To that case he always refers as "the affair of the Grey House." The house bears a different name in the annals of more than one scientific society, and much controversy has raged over the strange details of a story that seems to open up a new province of fantastic horror. Papers and treatises have been written about it in almost every European language, and many dismaying facts of a somewhat analogous nature have thus been brought to light. There was some hesitation at first about laying this matter—backed as it is by an explanation, which, though terrible, is not altogether unsupported—before the public, but it has finally been decided to incorporate it in the present series.

During the dry summer of 1893, Mr. Low happened to be staying in a lonely village on the coast of Devon. He was deeply immersed in some antiquarian work connected with the old Norse calendars, and therefore limited his acquaintance in the neighbourhood to one individual, a Dr. Fremantle, who, besides being a medical man, was a botanist of some note.

One afternoon, when driving together, Mr. Low and Dr. Fremantle passed through a valley which nestled cup-like in the higher ground a few miles inland. As they passed along a deep, steep Lane with overhanging hedges they caught a glimpse, through a break in the leaves, of a grey gable peeping out between the horizontal branches of a cedar.

Flaxman Low remarked upon it to his companion.

"That's young Montesson's house," answered Fremantle, "and it bears a very sinister reputation. Nothing in your line, though," with a smile. "Indeed, no ghost would lend the same hideous associations to the place it now possesses as the result of a succession of mysterious murders that have been committed there."

"The grounds seem neglected. I don't remember to have seen such rank growth anywhere."

"Certainly not inside the British Isles," returned Fremantle. "The estate is left to take care of itself, partly because Montesson won't live there, partly because it is impossible to find labourers to work near the house. Our warm, damp climate and this sheltered position give rise to extraordinary luxuriance of growth. A stream runs along the bottom, and I expect all the low-lying land, where you see that belt of yellow African grass, is little better than a morass now."

Fremantle drew up as they gained the top of the slope. From there they could overlook the tangle of vegetation, dimmed by a rising mist, which surrounded and almost hid the roof of the Grey House.

"Yes," said Fremantle, in answer to an observation of Mr. Low, "Montesson's guardian, who lived here and looked after the property for him, turned the place into a subtropical garden. It used to be one of my chief pleasures to wander about here, but since my marriage my wife objects to my doing so, on account of the tales she has heard."

"What is the danger?"

"Death!" replied Fremantle shortly.

"What form of death? Malaria?"

"No disease at all, my dear fellow. The persons who die at the Grey House are hanged by the neck until they are dead!"

"Hanged?" repeated Flaxman Low in surprise.

"Yes, hanged. Not only strangled, but suspended, as the marks on the necks show. If there were any hint of a ghost in it you might investigate—Montesson would be only too grateful if you could fathom the mystery."

"Tell me something more definite."

"I'll tell you what has happened in my own knowledge. Montesson's father died some fifteen years ago and left him to the guardianship of a cousin named Lampurt, who, as I told you, was a horticulturist, and planted the place with a wonderful variety of foreign shrubs and flowers. Lampurt had a bad name in the county, and his appearance was certainly against him—a squint-eyed, pig-faced fellow, who sidled along like a crab, and could not look you in the face. He died suddenly."

"Was he hanged? Or did he hang himself?"

"Neither, in this case. He dropped in a kind of fit, right up in front of the house, while he was engaged in planting some new acquisition. Had it not been for the evidence of the persons who were present at the time, I should have said his death resulted from some tremendous mental shock. But his relation, Mrs. Montesson, and the gardener agreed in saying that he was not exerting himself unduly, and that he had had no disturbing news. He was a healthy man, and I could see no sufficient reason for his death. He was simply gardening, and had apparently pricked himself with a nail, for he had a spot of blood upon his forefinger.

"After that all went well for a couple of years, when, during the summer holidays, the trouble began. Montesson must have been about sixteen at the time, and had a tutor with him. His mother and sister—a pretty girl rather older than himself—were also here. One morning the girl was found lying on the gravel under her window, quite dead. I was sent for, and, upon examination, discovered the extraordinary fact that she had been hanged!"

"Murder?"

"Of course, though we could find no trace of the murderer. The girl had been taken from her bedroom and hanged. Then the rope was removed, and she was thrown in a heap under her window. The crime caused a tremendous sensation in the neighbourhood, and the police were busy for a long time, but nothing came of their inquiries.

"About a fortnight later, Platt, the tutor, sat up smoking at the open study window. In the morning he was found lying out over the sill. There could be no mistake as to how he met his death, for in addition to the deep line round his throat, his neck was broken as neatly as they could have done it at Newgate! As in the other case, there was nothing to show how he came by his death, no rope, no trace of footsteps or any struggle to lead one to suspect the presence of another person or persons. Yet from the facts it could not have been suicide."

"I see you had some suspicion of your own," said Flaxman Low.

"Well, yes, I had. But time has passed, and I now think I must have been mistaken. I must explain that the branches of the cedar you saw jut to within a few feet of the windows of the rooms occupied by Miss Montesson and Platt respectively at the time of death. I told you there were no traces of any one having approached the house. It therefore struck me that some active person might have leaped from the cedar into the open windows and escaped in the same way, for the windows open vertically, and when both leaves are thrown back there is a large aperture. But the murders were so purposeless and disconnected that they suggested irresponsible agency. I recollected Poe's story of the Rue Morgue, where, you remember, the crimes were committed by an ourang-outang. It seemed to me possible that Lampurt, who was of a morose and strange temper, might, among other things, have secretly imported an ape and turned it loose in the woods. I had a thorough search made in the park and grounds, but we found nothing, and I have long ago abandoned the theory."

Low thought silently over the story for some time, then he asked for the dates of the three deaths. Fremantle answered categorically, and it appeared that all had taken place about the same season of the year—during summer, in fact. Upon this Mr. Low made an offer to investigate the affair on psychical lines, if Montesson made no objection. In answer to this message Montesson took the next train down to Devon, and begged to be allowed to accompany Mr. Low in his inquiries.

Flaxman Low quickly saw that Montesson might prove a very useful companion. He was a blonde, heavily-built man, and plainly possessed of a strong will and temper. Low put aside his books and went off at once with Montesson to have a closer look at the Grey House while the daylight lasted.

It is difficult to give any adequate impression of the teeming exuberance of wild and tangled growth through which they had to cut their way. Young, lush, sappy leafage overlay and half disguised the dank rottenness of the older vegetation beneath. After wading more than breast-high through the matted reeds, below which the spreading stream was fast reducing the land to a swamp, they emerged into a fairly open space that had once been the lawn round the house.

Here brambles and lusty weeds now grew abundantly under the untended trees. Curious shrubs and plants flourished here and there. As they came up a stoat sneaked away by a narrow footpath, nettle-grown and caked with damp, which led past blackened bushes round the house. Otherwise the place was deserted, not a leaf seemed to move in the windless heat of the afternoon. The squat, grey face of the house was scarred across by a dark-leaved creeper, hung with orchid-like red blossoms, a little to the left of which Low noticed the cedar mentioned by Dr. Fremantle.

Low drew up at the weed-twisted, sunken little gate that gave upon the lawns, and spoke for the first time.

"Tell me about it," and he nodded towards the house.

Montesson repeated the story already told, but added further details. "From here," went on Montesson, "you can see the exact spot where all these things took place. The upper of these two windows, surrounded by the creeper and under the shadow of the cedar, belonged to my sister's room; the lower is that of the study where Platt died. The gravel path below ran the whole length of the house, but it is now overgrown. Has Fremantle told you of Lawrence?"

Low shook his head.

"I hate the very sight of the place!" said Montesson hoarsely; "the mystery and the horror of it all seem in my blood. I can't forget!—My mother left on the day of Platt's death, and has never been here since. But when I came of age I resolved to make another attempt to live here, meaning to sift the past if I got the chance of doing so. I had the grounds cleared about the house, and after leaving Oxford came down with a man of my own year, called Lawrence. We spent the Easter vacation here reading, and all went right enough. Meanwhile I had the house examined, thinking there might be a secret entrance or room, but nothing of the kind exists. This house is not haunted. Nothing has ever been seen or heard of a supernatural character—nothing but the same awful repetition of blind murder!"

After a few seconds he resumed.

"During the following summer Lawrence came down with me again. One hot evening we were smoking as we walked up and down the gravel under the windows. It was bright moonlight, and I remember the heavy scent of those red flowers——" Montesson glanced round him strangely.

"I went in to fetch a cigar. It took me some minutes to find the box I wanted, and to light the cigar. When I came out, Lawrence lay crumpled up as if he had fallen from a height, and he was dead. Round his neck was the same bluish line I had seen in the two other cases. You can understand what it was to leave the man not five minutes before, in health and strength, and to come back to find him dead—hanged, to judge from appearances! But as usual, no trace of rope or struggle or murderer!"

After some further talk, Mr. Low proposed to go into the house. It had evidently been deserted in haste. In the room once occupied by Miss Montesson her girlish treasures still lay about, dusty, moth-eaten, and discoloured. Montesson paused on the threshold.

"Poor little Fan! It's just as she left it!" he said hurriedly.

The cedar outside threw a gloomy shade into the room, and the fantastic red blossoms drooped motionless in the stagnant air.

"Was the window open when your sister was found?" inquired Low after he had examined the room.

"Yes, it was hot weather—early in August. This room has not been occupied since. After Platt's affair, I have always avoided this side of the house, so that it was only by chance Lawrence and I came round to this part of the lawn to smoke."

"Then we may suppose that the danger, whatever it is, exists on this side of the house only?"

"So it seems," replied Montesson.

"Your sister was last seen alive in this room? Platt in the room directly below? and your friend—what of him?"

"Lawrence was lying on the gravel path just under the study window. All of them have died under the shadow of the cedar. Did Fremantle give you his idea? Poor Lawrence's death disposed of that theory. No big ape could live in England all those five years in the open, and in any case it must have been seen sometime in the interval."

"I think so," replied Low abstractedly. "Now as to what we must do to try and get at the meaning of all this. Do you feel equal, considering all you have gone through in this house, do you feel equal to remaining here with me for a night or two?"

Montesson again glanced over his shoulder nervously.

"Yes," he said. "I know my nerves are not as stiff and steady as they should be, but I'll stand by you—especially as you would not find another man about here willing to run the risk. You see it is not a ghost or any fanciful trouble, it means a real danger. Think over it, Mr. Low, before you undertake so hazardous an attempt."

Low looked into the blue eyes Montesson had fixed upon him. They were weary, anxious eyes, and, taken in combination with his compressed lips and square chin, told Low of the struggle this man constantly endured between his shaken nervous system and the strong will that mastered it.

"If you'll stand by me, I'll try to get to the bottom of it," said Low.

"I wonder if I should allow you to risk your life in this way?" returned Montesson, passing his hand over his prematurely-lined forehead.

"Why not? Besides, it is my own wish. As for risking our lives—it is for the good of mankind."

"I can't say I see it in that light," said Montesson, in surprise.

"If we lose our lives it will be in the effort to make another spot of earth clean and wholesome and safe for men to live on. Our duty to the public requires us to run a murderer to earth. Here we have a murderous power of some subtle kind; is it not quite as much our duty to destroy it if we can, even at risk to ourselves?"

The result of this conversation was an arrangement to pass the night at the Grey House. About ten o'clock they set out, intending to follow the path they had more or less successfully cleared for themselves in the afternoon. By Flaxman Low's advice, Montesson carried a long knife. The night was unusually hot and still, and lit only by a thin moon as they made their way along, stumbling over matted weeds and roots, and literally feeling for the path, until they came to the little gate by the lawn. There they stopped a moment to look at the house, standing out among its strange sea of overgrowth, the dim moon low on the horizon, glinting palely upon the windows and over the deserted countryside. As they waited a night-bird hooted and flapped its way across the open.

At any moment they might be at handgrips with the mysterious power of death which haunted the place. The warm lush-scented air and the sinister shadows seemed charged with some ominous influence. As they drew near the house Low perceived a sweet, heavy odour.

"What is it?" he asked.

"It comes from those scarlet flowers. It's unbearable! Lampurt imported the thing," replied Montesson irritably.

"Which room will you spend the night in?" asked Low as they gained the hall.

Montesson hesitated. "Have you ever heard the expression 'grey with fear'?" he said, laughing in the dark; "I'm that!"

Low did not like the laugh, it was only one remove, and that a very little one, from hysteria.

"We won't find out much unless we each remain alone, and with open windows as they did," said Low.

Montesson shook himself.

"No, I suppose not. *They* were each alone when—— Good night, I'll call if anything happens, and you must do the same for me. For Heaven's sake, don't go to sleep!"

"And remember," added Low, "to cut at anything that touches you with your knife." Then he stood at the study door and listened to Montesson's heavy steps as they passed up the stairs, for he had elected to pass the night in his sister's room. Low heard him walk across the floor above and throw wide the window.

When Mr. Low turned into the study and tried to open the window there, he found it impossible to do so, the creeper outside had fastened upon the woodwork, binding the sashes together. There was but one thing left for him to do, he must go outside and stand where Lawrence had stood on the fatal night. He let himself out softly, and went round to the south side of the house.

There he paced up and down in the shadows for perhaps an hour.

In the deceptive, iridescent moonlight a pallid head seemed to wag at him from the gloom below the cedar, but, moving towards it, he grasped only the yellow bunched blossom of a giant ragwort. Then he stood still and looked up into the branches above—the gnarled black branches, with their fringes of sticky, black leaves. Fremantle's theory of the ape passing stealthily among them to spring upon his victims found a sudden horror of possibility in Low's mind. He imagined the girl awaking in the brute's cruel hands——

Out upon the quiet brooding of the night broke a scream—or rather a roar, a harsh, jagged, pulsating roar, that ceased as abruptly as it had begun.

Without a moment's consideration, Mr. Low seized the branch nearest to him and, swinging himself up into the tree, he climbed with a frantic effort towards the window of Montesson's room, from which he was almost sure the sound had come. Being an unusually active and athletic man, he leaped from the branch towards the open window, and fell headlong in upon the floor. As he did so, something seemed to pass him, something swift and sinuous that might have been a snake, and disappeared out of the window!

Remembering a candle on the toilet table, he lit it when he regained his feet and looked about him.

Montesson lay on the floor "crumpled up," as he had himself described Lawrence's position. Low recalled this with misgiving as he hurried to his side. A dark smear like blood was on Montesson's cheek, but though unconscious, he was still alive. Low lifted him on to the bed and did what he could to rouse him, but without success. He lay rigid, breathing the slow, almost imperceptible, respiration of deep stupor.

Low was about to go to the window, when the candle suddenly went out, and he was left in the increasing darkness, to all intents alone, to face an unknown though tangible assailant.

Silence had again fallen upon the house—that is, the silence of night, and woodlands, and many-folded leafage, and the things that go by night. He stood by the window and listened. His senses were acute and throbbing; he felt as if he could hear for miles. The scent of the scarlet blossoms rose like deadening fumes into his brain, and he drew away from the window, and, feeling strangely spent, threw himself upon a couch. Then he drew out the knife at his belt, and strung himself up to watchfulness with an effort.

He knew that the attack he had to expect would be likely to come from the direction of the window. He saw the faint, swimming moonlight that fell through the leaves and tendrils of the creeper fade slowly away. Probably clouds were coming up over the sky, for the steamy heat was even more oppressive.

The low window-sill was scarcely more than a foot above the floor, and presently he fancied something was moving along the carpet among the entangling shadows of the leaves, but the darkness was now intensified, and he could not be sure. Montesson's breathing had become quieter. It was the dead hour of the night; hardly a sound was to be heard.

Suddenly Low felt a soft touch upon his knee. His whole consciousness had been so absorbed in the act of listening that this unexpected appeal to another sense startled him. Here and there—rapid, soft, and light—the touches passed over his body. It might have been some animal nosing about him in the dark. Then a smooth, cold touch fell upon his cheek.

Low sprang up, and slashed about him in the darkness with his knife.

In that instant the thing closed with him—a flexuous, snaky thing that flung its coils about his limbs and body in one swift spring like a curling whiplash!

Flaxman Low was all but helpless in the winding grasp of what?—the tentacles of some strange creature? or was it some great snake, this sentient thing that was feeling for his throat? There was not an instant to lose. The knife was pressed against his body; with a violent effort he drew it sharply, edge outwards, against the tightening coils. A spurt of clammy fluid fell upon his hand, and the thing loosed and fell away from him into the stifling gloom. . . .

In the morning Montesson came to himself in one of the lower rooms at the other side of the house. Fremantle was beside him.

"What's the matter?" he asked. "Ah, I remember now. There's Low. It has beaten us again, Fremantle! It is hopeless. I don't know what happened—I was not asleep, when I found myself seized, lifted up, drawn towards the window, and strangled by living ropes. Look at Low!" he went on harshly, raising himself. "Why, man, you're all over blood!"

Flaxman Low glanced down at his hands.

"Looks like it," he said.

"It has beaten even you, Low!" went on Montesson. "There is something much more terrible and tangible than a ghost in this cursed house! See here!"

He pulled down his collar. A faint bluish circle with suffused dots was drawn round his throat.

"It is some deadly species of snake," exclaimed Fremantle.

Low sat down astride a chair thoughtfully.

"I'm sorry to disagree with both of you. But I am inclined to think it is not a snake, and, on the other hand, I fancy it has a great deal to do with what we may roughly call a ghost. The whole evidence points in only one direction."

"You mustn't let your prejudice in favour of psychical problems run away with your reason," said Fremantle drily. "Has a ghost actual, palpable power?—to go further, has it blood?"

Montesson, who had been looking at his neck in the glass, turned quickly. "It's some horrible thing in nature! Something between a snake and an octopus! What do you say to it, Low?"

Low looked up gravely.

"In spite of Fremantle's objections, the steps from beginning to end are very clear."

Fremantle and Montesson exchanged a glance of incredulity.

"My dear fellow, much learning has warped your mind," said Fremantle, with an embarrassed laugh.

"First of all," continued Low, "we know where all the deaths have occurred."

"To speak precisely, they have all occurred in different places," interposed Fremantle.

"True; but within a strictly limited area. The slight differences have been of material help to me. In all cases they have occurred in the vicinity of one thing."

"The cedar!" cried Montesson, with some excitement.

"That was my first idea—now I refer to the wall. Will you tell me the probable weight of Lawrence and Platt at the date of death?"

"Platt was a small man—perhaps under nine stone. Lawrence, though much taller, was thin, and could not have weighed more than eleven. As for poor little Fan, she was only a slip of a girl."

"Three people have been killed—one has escaped. In what way do you differ from the others, Montesson?" asked Low.

"If you mean I'm heavier, I certainly am. I scale something like fifteen. But what has that to do with it?"

"Everything. The coils have evidently not sufficient compressive power to destroy life by strangulation simply—there must be suspension as well. You were simply too heavy for them to tackle."

"Coils of what?"

"Of this." Low held up a tapering, reddish-brown tendon or line, which had red-curved triangular teeth set on it at intervals.

The two other men stared at this object, and then Montesson burst out: "The creeper on the wall!" he said, in a tone of disappointment. "It couldn't be! Besides, has a plant blood?"

"Let us go and look at it," said Low. "This creeper has never been cut because it withers away every winter to the ground and grows again in the spring. Look here!" He took out his knife and cut a leathery shoot. A crimson stain spurted out on his cuff. "The only person, as far as I can gather, who cut this plant was Mr. Lampurt in nailing it to the wall. He died of shock when he saw the red stain on his finger, as he knew something of its deadly properties. But though stupefying—as your condition last night proved, Montesson—they are not fatal. Even to stupefy they must get into the blood. Now the deaths have all occurred within reach of the tendrils of this plant. And all have happened at the same season of the year, that is to say, at the time when it attains its full annual strength and growth. Another point in favour of Montesson's escape was the dryness of the season. The growth is not quite so good as usual this summer, is it?"

"No; the tendrils are thinner—a good deal thinner and smaller."

"Just so. Therefore your weight saved you, though you were stupefied by the punctures of the thorns. I feared that, and warned you to use your knife."

"But the brain of the thing?" cried Fremantle. "Why, man, has a plant will and knowledge and malevolence?"

"Not of itself, as I believe," answered Low. "Perhaps you will prefer to attribute much to the long arm of coincidence, but the explanation I can offer is one that has for ages been held by occultists in other countries. Pythagoras and others have taught that the forms of incarnation change as the soul raises or debases itself during each spell of Life. Connect with this the belief of the Brahmins, and I may add of various African tribes, that an earthbound spirit, at the moment of a premature or sudden death, may pass into plants or trees of certain species, by virtue of an inherent attraction possessed by these plants for such entities. To go further, it is said that these degraded souls are given intervals during which they have power of voluntary action to do good or evil, and such action has influence on their future incarnations."

"What do you mean? What do you intend us to believe?" Montesson said, and stopped.

"It is hard to put it into words in these latter days of unbelief," said Low, "but the evidence goes to show that a man—presumably not a good man—dies a sudden death near this plant, even inoculated with its sap. Fremantle knows this plant to be a Malayan creeper, belonging to a family that possess strange powers and properties. I may recall the old story of the upas-tree, and more lately still the murder-tree discovered near Kolwe, in East Africa, by Herr Boltze. There are also other instances."

"It is incredible!" said Fremantle almost angrily.

"I don't ask you to believe it," said Flaxman Low quietly, "I only tell you such beliefs exist. Montesson can do something towards proving my theory. Let him have the plant destroyed, and judge by results."

The tendril of the creeper severed by Mr. Low in his struggle was presented by him to the authorities at Kew.

Mr. Montesson has acted upon Mr. Flaxman Low's suggestions. The Grey House is now occupied and safe, and it is a strange fact that no plant, not even the hardy ivy, will live where the red-blossomed creeper once grew.

THE STORY OF YAND MANOR HOUSE

Looking through the notes of Mr. Flaxman Low, one sometimes catches through the steel-blue hardness of facts the pink flush of romance, or more often the black corner of a horror unnameable. The following story may serve as an instance of the latter. Mr. Low not only unravelled the mystery at Yand, but at the same time justified his life-work to M. Thierry, the well-known French critic and philosopher.

At the end of a long conversation, M. Thierry, arguing from his own standpoint as a materialist, had said—

"The factor in the human economy which you call 'soul' cannot be placed."

"I admit that," replied Low. "Yet, when a man dies, is there not one factor unaccounted for in the change that comes upon him? Yes! For though his body still exists, it rapidly falls to pieces, which proves that that has gone which held it together."

The Frenchman laughed, and shifted his ground.

"Well, for my part, I don't believe in ghosts! Spirit manifestations, occult phenomena—is not this the ashbin into which a certain clique shoot everything they cannot understand, or for which they fail to account?"

"Then what should you say to me, Monsieur, if I told you that I have passed a good portion of my life in investigating this particular ashbin, and have been lucky enough to sort a small part of its contents with tolerable success?" replied Flaxman Low.

"The subject is doubtless interesting—but I should like to have some personal experience in the matter," said Thierry dubiously.

"I am at present investigating a most singular case," said Low. "Have you a day or two to spare?"

Thierry thought for a minute or more.

"I am grateful," he replied. "But, forgive me, is it a convincing ghost?"

"Come with me to Yand and see. I have been there once already, and came away for the purpose of procuring information from MSS. to which I have the privilege of access, for I confess that the phenomena at Yand lie altogether outside any former experience of mine."

Low sank back into his chair with his hands clasped behind his head—a favourite position of his—and the smoke of his long pipe curled up lazily into the golden face of an Isis, which stood behind him on a bracket. Thierry, glancing across, was struck by the strange likeness between the faces of the Egyptian goddess and this scientist of the nineteenth century. On both rested the calm, mysterious abstraction of some unfathomable thought. As he looked, he decided.

"I have three days to place at your disposal."

"I thank you heartily," replied Low. "To be associated with so brilliant a logician as yourself in an inquiry of this nature is more than I could have hoped for! The material with which I have to deal is so elusive, the whole subject is wrapped in such obscurity and hampered by so much prejudice, that I can find few really qualified persons who care to approach these investigations seriously. I go down to Yand this evening, and hope not to leave without clearing up the mystery. You will accompany me?"

"Most certainly. Meanwhile pray tell me something of the affair."

"Briefly the story is as follows. Some weeks ago I went to Yand Manor House at the request of the owner, Sir George Blackburton, to see what I could make of the events which took place there. All they complain of is the impossibility of remaining in one room—the dining-room."

"What then is he like, this M. le Spook?" asked the Frenchman, laughing.

"No one has ever seen him, or for that matter heard him."

"Then how——"

"You can't see him, nor hear him, nor smell him," went on Low, "but you can feel him and—taste him!"

"*Mon Dieu!* But this is singular! Is he then of so bad a flavour?"

"You shall taste for yourself," answered Flaxman Low, smiling. "After a certain hour no one can remain in the room, they are simply crowded out."

"But who crowds them out?" asked Thierry.

"That is just what I hope we may discover to-night or to-morrow."

The last train that night dropped Mr. Flaxman Low and his companion at a little station near Yand. It was late, but a trap in waiting soon carried them to the Manor

House. The big bulk of the building stood up in absolute blackness before them.

"Blackburton was to have met us, but I suppose he has not yet arrived," said Low. "Hullo! the door is open," he added, as he stepped into the hall.

Beyond a dividing curtain they now perceived a light. Passing behind this curtain they found themselves at the end of the long hall, the wide staircase opening up in front of them.

"But who is this?" exclaimed Thierry.

Swaying and stumbling at every step, there tottered slowly down the stairs the figure of a man. He looked as if he had been drinking, his face was livid, and his eyes sunk into his head.

"Thank Heaven you've come! I heard you outside," he said in a weak voice.

"It's Sir George Blackburton," said Low, as the man lurched forward and pitched into his arms.

They laid him down on the rugs and tried to restore consciousness.

"He has the air of being drunk, but it is not so," remarked Thierry. "Monsieur has had a bad shock of the nerves. See the pulses drumming in his throat."

In a few minutes Blackburton opened his eyes and staggered to his feet.

"Come. I could not remain there alone. Come quickly."

They went rapidly across the hall, Blackburton leading the way down a wide passage to a double-leaved door, which, after a perceptible pause, he threw open, and they all entered together.

On the great table in the centre stood an extinguished lamp, some scattered food, and a big, lighted candle. But the eyes of all three men passed at once to a dark recess beside the heavy, carved chimneypiece, where a rigid shape sat perched on the back of a huge, oak chair.

Flaxman Low snatched up the candle and crossed the room towards it.

On the top of the chair, with his feet upon the arms, sat a powerfully built young man huddled up. His mouth was open, and his eyes twisted upwards. Nothing further could be seen from below but the ghastly pallor of cheek and throat.

"Who is this?" cried Low. Then he laid his hand gently on the man's knee.

At the touch the figure collapsed in a heap upon the floor, the gaping, set, terrified face turned up to theirs.

"He's dead!" said Low, after a hasty examination. "I should say he's been dead some hours."

"O Lord! Poor Batty!" groaned Sir George, who was entirely unnerved. "I'm glad you've come, Low."

"Who is he?" said Thierry, "and what was he doing here?"

"He's a gamekeeper of mine. He was always anxious to try conclusions with the ghost, and last night he begged me to lock him in here with food for twenty-four hours. I was opposed to it, but then I thought if anything happened while he was in here alone, it would interest you. Who could imagine it would end like this?"

"When did you find him?" asked Low.

"I only got here from my mother's half an hour ago. I turned on the light in the hall and came in here with a candle. As I entered the room, the candle went out, and—and—I think I must be going mad."

"Tell us everything you saw," urged Low.

"You will think I am beside myself; but as the light went out, and I sank almost paralysed into an armchair, I saw two barred eyes looking at me!"

"Barred eyes? What do you mean?"

"Eyes that looked at me through thin vertical bars, like the bars of a cage. What's that?"

With a smothered yell Sir George sprang back. He had approached the dead man and declared something had brushed his face.

"You were standing on this spot under the overmantel. I will remain here. Meantime, my dear Thierry, I feel sure you will help Sir George to carry this poor fellow to some more suitable place," said Flaxman Low.

When the dead body of the young gamekeeper had been carried out, Low passed slowly round and about the room. At length he stood under the old carved overmantel, which reached to the ceiling and projected boldly forward in quaint heads of satyrs and animals. One of these on the side nearest the recess represented a griffin with a fanged mouth. Sir George had been standing directly below this at the moment when he felt the touch on his face. Now alone in the dim, wide room, Flaxman Low stood on the same spot and waited. The candle threw its dull yellow rays on the shadows, which seemed to gather closer and wait also. Presently a distant door banged, and Low, leaning forward to listen, distinctly felt something on the back of his neck!

He swung round. There was nothing! He searched carefully on all sides, then put his hand up to the griffin's head. Again came the same soft touch, this time upon his hand, as if something had floated past on the air.

This was definite. The griffin's head located it. Taking the candle to examine more closely, Low found four long black hairs depending from the jagged fangs. He was detaching them when Thierry reappeared.

"We must get Sir George away as soon as possible," he said.

"Yes, we must take him away, I fear," agreed Low. "Our investigation must be put off till to-morrow."

On the following day they returned to Yand. It was a large country-house, pretty and old-fashioned, with latticed windows and deep gables, that looked out between tall shrubs and across lawns set with beaupots, where peacocks sunned themselves on the velvet turf. The church spire peered over the trees at one side; and an old wall covered with ivy and creeping plants, and pierced at intervals with arches, alone separated the gardens from the churchyard.

The haunted room lay at the back of the house. It was square and handsome, and furnished in the style of the last century. The oak overmantel reached to the ceiling, and a wide window, which almost filled one side of the room, gave a view of the west door of the church.

Low stood for a moment at the open window, looking out at the level sunlight which flooded the lawns and parterres.

"See that door sunk in the church wall to the left?" said Sir George's voice at his elbow. "That is the door of the family vault. Cheerful outlook, isn't it?"

"I should like to walk across there presently," remarked Low.

"What! Into the vault?" asked Sir George, with a harsh laugh. "I'll take you, if you like. Anything else I can show you or tell you?"

"Yes. Last night I found this hanging from the griffin's head," said Low, producing the thin wisp of black hair. "It must have touched your cheek as you stood below. Do you know to whom it can belong?"

"It's a woman's hair! No; the only woman who has been in this room to my knowledge for months is an old servant with grey hair who cleans it," returned Blackburton. "I'm sure it was not here when I locked Batty in."

"It is human hair, exceedingly coarse, and long uncut," said Low; "but it is not necessarily a woman's."

"It is not mine, at any rate, for I'm sandy, and poor Batty was fair. Good night; I'll come round for you in the morning."

Presently, when the night closed in, Thierry and Low settled down in the haunted room to await developments. They smoked and talked deep into the night. A big lamp burned brightly on the table, and the surroundings looked homely and desirable.

Thierry made a remark to that effect, adding that perhaps the ghost might see fit to omit his usual visit.

"Experience goes to prove that ghosts have a cunning habit of choosing persons either credulous or excitable to experiment upon," he added.

To M. Thierry's surprise, Flaxman Low agreed with him.

"They certainly choose suitable persons," he said; "that is, not credulous persons, but those whose senses are sufficiently keen to detect the presence of a spirit. In my own investigations, I try to eliminate what you would call the supernatural element. I deal with these mysterious affairs as far as possible on material lines."

"Then what do you say of Batty's death? He died of fright—simply."

"I hardly think so. The manner of his death agrees in a peculiar manner with what we know of the terrible history of this room. He died of fright and pressure combined. Did you hear the doctor's remark? It was significant. He said: 'The indications are precisely those I have observed in persons who have been crushed and killed in a crowd!'"

"That is sufficiently curious, I allow. I see that it is already past two o'clock. I am thirsty; I will have a little seltzer." Thierry rose from his chair, and, going to the sideboard, drew a tumblerful from the syphon. "Pah! What an abominable taste!"

"What? The seltzer?"

"Not at all!" returned the Frenchman irritably. "I have not touched it yet. Some horrible fly has flown into my mouth, I suppose. Pah! Disgusting!"

"What is it like?" asked Flaxman Low, who was at the moment wiping his own mouth with his handkerchief.

"Like? As if some repulsive fungus had burst in the mouth."

"Exactly. I perceive it also. I hope you are about to be convinced."

"What?" exclaimed Thierry, turning his big figure round and staring at Low. "You don't mean——"

As he spoke the lamp suddenly went out.

"Why, then, have you put the lamp out at such a moment?" cried Thierry.

"I have not put it out. Light the candle beside you on the table."

Low heard the Frenchman's grunt of satisfaction as he found the candle, then the scratch of a match. It spluttered and went out. Another match and another behaved in the same manner, while Thierry swore freely under his breath.

"Let me have your matches, Monsieur Flaxman; mine are, no doubt, damp," he said at last.

Low rose to feel his way across the room. The darkness was dense.

"It is the darkness of Egypt—it may be felt. Where then are you, my dear friend?" he heard Thierry saying, but the voice seemed a long way off.

"I am coming," he answered, "but it's so hard to get along."

After Low had spoken the words, their meaning struck him. He paused, and tried to realise in what part of the room he was. The silence was profound, and the growing sense of oppression seemed like a nightmare. Thierry's voice sounded again, faint and receding.

"I am suffocating. Monsieur Flaxman, where are you? I am near the door. Ach!"

A strangling bellow of pain and fear followed, that scarcely reached Low through the thickening atmosphere.

"Thierry, what is the matter with you?" he shouted. "Open the door."

But there was no answer. What had become of Thierry in that hideous, clogging gloom? Was he also dead, crushed in some ghastly fashion against the wall? What was this?

The air had become palpable to the touch, heavy, repulsive, with the sensation of cold humid flesh!

Low pushed out his hands with a mad longing to touch a table, a chair, anything but this clammy, swelling softness that thrust itself upon him from every side, baffling him and filling his grasp.

He knew now that he was absolutely alone—struggling against what?

His feet were slipping in his wild efforts to feel the floor—the dank flesh was creeping upon his neck, his cheek—his breath came short and labouring as the pressure swung him gently to and fro, helpless, nauseated!

The clammy flesh crowded upon him like the bulk of some fat, horrible creature; then came a stinging pain on the cheek. Low clutched at something: there was a crash and a rush of air——

The next sensation of which Mr. Flaxman Low was conscious was one of deathly sickness. He was lying on wet grass, the wind blowing over him, and all the clean, wholesome smells of the open air in his nostrils.

He sat up and looked about him. Dawn was breaking windily in the east, and by its light he saw that he was on the lawn of Yand Manor House. The latticed window of the haunted room above him was open. He tried to remember what had happened. He took stock of himself, in fact, and slowly felt that he still held something clutched in his right hand—something dark-coloured, slender, and twisted. It might have been a long shred of bark or the cast skin of an adder—it was impossible to see in the dim light.

After an interval the recollection of Thierry recurred to him. Scrambling to his feet, he raised himself to the window sill and looked in. Contrary to his expectation, there was no upsetting of furniture; everything remained in position as when the lamp went out. His own chair and the one Thierry had occupied were just as when they had risen from them. But there was no sign of Thierry.

Low jumped in by the window. There was the tumbler full of seltzer, and the litter of matches about it. He took up Thierry's box of matches and struck a light. It flared, and he lit the candle with ease. In fact, everything about the room was perfectly normal; all the horrible conditions prevailing but a couple of hours ago had disappeared.

But where was Thierry? Carrying the lighted candle, he passed out of the door and searched in the adjoining rooms. In one of them, to his relief, he found the Frenchman sleeping profoundly in an armchair.

Low touched his arm. Thierry leapt to his feet, fending off an imaginary blow with his arm. Then he turned his scared face on Low.

"What! You, Monsieur Flaxman! How have you escaped?"

"I should rather ask you how you escaped," said Low, smiling at the havoc the night's experiences had worked in his friend's looks and spirits.

"I was crowded out of the room against the door. That infernal thing—what was it?—with its damp, swelling flesh, inclosed me!" A shudder of disgust stopped him. "I was a fly in an aspic. I could not move. I sank into the stifling pulp. The air grew thick. I called to you, but your answers became inaudible. Then I was suddenly thrust against the door by a huge hand—it felt like one, at least. I had a struggle for my life, I was all but crushed, and then, I do not know how, I found myself outside the door. I shouted to you in vain. Therefore, as I could not help you, I came here, and—I will confess it, my dear friend—I locked and bolted the door. After some time I went again into the hall and listened; but, as I heard nothing, I resolved to wait until daylight and the return of Sir George."

"That's all right," said Low. "It was an experience worth having."

"But, no! Not for me! I do not envy you your researches into mysteries of this abominable description. I now comprehend perfectly that Sir George has lost his nerve if he has had to do with this horror. Besides, it is entirely impossible to explain these things."

At this moment they heard Sir George's arrival, and went out to meet him.

"I could not sleep all night for thinking of you!" exclaimed Blackburton on seeing them; "and I came along as soon as it was light. Something has happened?"

"But certainly something has happened," cried M. Thierry, shaking his head solemnly; "something of the most bizarre, of the most horrible! Monsieur Flaxman, you shall tell Sir George this story. You have been in that accursed room all the night, and remain alive to tell the tale!"

As Low came to the conclusion of the story Sir George suddenly exclaimed—

"You have met with some injury to your face, Mr. Low."

Low turned to the mirror. In the now strong light three parallel weals from eye to mouth could be seen.

"I remember a stinging pain like a lash on my cheek. What would you say these marks were caused by, Thierry?" asked Low.

Thierry looked at them and shook his head.

"No one in their senses would venture to offer any explanation of the occurrences of last night," he replied.

"Something of this sort, do you think?" asked Low again, putting down the object he held in his hand on the table.

Thierry took it up and described it aloud.

"A long and thin object of a brown and yellow colour, and twisted like a sabre-bladed corkscrew." Then he started slightly and glanced up at Low.

"It's a human nail, I imagine," suggested Low.

"But no human being has talons of this kind—except, perhaps, a Chinaman of high rank."

"There are no Chinamen about here, nor ever have been, to my knowledge," said Blackburton shortly. "I'm very much afraid that, in spite of all you have so bravely faced, we are no nearer to any rational explanation."

"On the contrary, I fancy I begin to see my way. I believe, after all, that I may be able to convert you, Thierry," said Flaxman Low.

"Convert me?"

"To a belief in the definite aim of my work. But you shall judge for yourself. What do you make of it so far? I claim that you know as much of the matter as I do."

"My dear, good friend, I make nothing of it," returned Thierry, shrugging his shoulders and spreading out his hands. "Here we have a tissue of unprecedented incidents that can be explained on no theory whatever."

"But this is definite," and Flaxman Low held up the blackened nail.

"And how do you propose to connect that nail with the black hairs—with the eyes that looked through the bars of a cage—the fate of Batty, with its symptoms of death by pressure and suffocation—our experience of swelling flesh, that something which filled and filled the room to the exclusion of all else? How are you going to account for these things by any kind of connected hypothesis?" asked Thierry, with a shade of irony.

"I mean to try," replied Low.

At lunch-time Thierry inquired how the theory was getting on.

"It progresses," answered Low. "By the way, Sir George, who lived in this house for some time prior to, say, 1840? He was a man—it may have been a woman, but, from the nature of his studies, I am inclined to think it was a man—who was deeply read in ancient necromancy, Eastern magic, mesmerism, and subjects of a kindred nature. And was he not buried in the vault you pointed out?"

"Do you know anything more about him?" asked Sir George in surprise.

"He was, I imagine," went on Flaxman Low reflectively, "hirsute and swarthy, probably a recluse, and suffered from a morbid and extravagant fear of death."

"How do you know all this?"

"I only asked about it. Am I right?"

"You have described my cousin, Sir Gilbert Blackburton, in every particular. I can show you his portrait in another room."

As they stood looking at the painting of Sir Gilbert Blackburton, with his long melancholy olive face and thick black beard, Sir George went on: "My grandfather succeeded him at Yand. I have often heard my father speak of Sir Gilbert, and his strange studies and extraordinary fear of death. Oddly enough, in the end he died rather suddenly, while he was still hale and strong. He predicted his own approaching death, and had a doctor in attendance for a week or two before he died. He was placed in a coffin he had had made on some plan of his own, and buried in the vault. His death occurred in 1842 or 1843. If you care to see them, I can show you some of his papers, which may interest you."

Mr. Flaxman Low spent the afternoon over the papers. When evening came, he rose from his work with a sigh of content, stretched himself, and joined Thierry and Sir George in the garden.

They dined at Lady Blackburton's, and it was late before Sir George found himself alone with Mr. Flaxman Low and his friend.

"Have you formed any opinion about the thing which haunts the Manor House?" he asked anxiously.

Thierry elaborated a cigarette, crossed his legs, and added—

"If you have in truth come to any definite conclusion, pray let us hear it, my dear Monsieur Flaxman."

"I have reached a very definite and satisfactory conclusion," replied Low. "The Manor House is haunted by Sir Gilbert Blackburton, who died, or, rather, who seemed to die, on the 15th of August 1842."

"Nonsense! The nail fifteen inches long at least—how do you connect it with Sir Gilbert?" asked Blackburton testily.

"I am convinced that it belonged to Sir Gilbert," Low answered.

"But the long black hair like a woman's?"

"Dissolution in the case of Sir Gilbert was not complete—not consummated, so to speak—as I hope to show you later. Even in the case of dead persons the hair and nails have been known to grow. By a rough calculation as to the growth of nails in such cases, I was enabled to indicate approximately the date of Sir Gilbert's death. The hair, too, grew on his head."

"But the barred eyes? I saw them myself!" exclaimed the young man.

"The eyelashes grow also. You follow me?"

"You have, I presume, some theory in connection with this?" observed Thierry. "It must be a very curious one."

"Sir Gilbert, in his fear of death, appears to have mastered and elaborated a strange and ancient formula by which the grosser factors of the body being eliminated, the more ethereal portions continue to retain the spirit, and the body is thus preserved from absolute disintegration.

In this manner true death may be indefinitely deferred. Secure from the ordinary chances and changes of existence, the spiritualised body could retain a modified life practically for ever."

"This is a most extraordinary idea, my dear fellow," remarked Thierry.

"But why should Sir Gilbert haunt the Manor House, and one special room?"

"The tendency of spirits to return to the old haunts of bodily life is almost universal. We cannot yet explain the reason of this attraction of environment."

"But the expansion—the crowding substance which we ourselves felt? You cannot meet that difficulty," said Thierry persistently.

"Not as fully as I could wish, perhaps. But the power of expanding and contracting to a degree far beyond our comprehension is a well-known attribute of spiritualised matter."

"Wait one little moment, my dear Monsieur Flaxman," broke in Thierry's voice after an interval; "this is very clever and ingenious indeed. As a theory, I give it my sincere admiration. But proof—proof is what we now demand."

Flaxman Low looked at the two steadily incredulous faces.

"This," he said slowly, "is the hair of Sir Gilbert Blackburton, and this nail is from the little finger of his left hand. You can prove my assertion by opening the coffin."

Sir George, who was pacing up and down the room impatiently, drew up.

"I don't like it at all, Mr. Low, I tell you frankly. I don't like it at all. I see no object in violating the coffin. I am not concerned to verify this unpleasant theory of yours. I have only one desire; I want to get rid of this haunting presence, whatever it is."

"If I am right," replied Low, "the opening of the coffin and exposure of the remains to strong sunshine for a short time will free you for ever from this presence. . . ."

In the early morning, when the summer sun struck warmly on the lawns of Yand, the three men carried the coffin from the vault to a quiet spot among the shrubs, where, secure from observation, they raised the lid.

Within the coffin lay the semblance of Gilbert Blackburton, maned to the ears with long and coarse black hair. Matted eyelashes swept the fallen cheeks, and beside the body stretched the bony hands, each with its dependent sheaf of switch-like nails. Low bent over and raised the left hand gingerly.

The little finger was without a nail!

Two hours later they came back and looked again. The sun had in the meantime done its work; nothing remained but a fleshless skeleton and a few half-rotten shreds of clothing.

The ghost of Yand Manor House has never since been heard of.

When Thierry bade Flaxman Low good-bye, he said—

"In time, my dear Monsieur Flaxman, you will add another to our sciences. You establish your facts too well for my peace of mind."

THE STORY OF SEVENS HALL

"It may be quite true," said Yarkindale gloomily; "all that I can answer is that we always die the same way. Some of us choose, or are driven, to one form of suicide, and some to another, but the result is alike. For three generations every man of my family has died by his own hand. I have not come to you hoping for help, Mr. Low; I merely want to tell the facts to a man who may possibly believe that we are not insane, that heredity and madness have nothing to do with our leaving the world; but that we are forced out of it by some external power acting upon us, I do not know how. If we inherit anything, it is clear-headedness and strength of will; but this curse of ours is stronger. That is all."

Flaxman Low kicked the fire into a blaze. It shone on the silver and china of the breakfast service, and on the sallow, despairing face of the man in the armchair opposite. He was still young, but already the cloud that rested upon his life had carved deep lines upon his forehead in addition to the long, tell-tale groove from mouth to nostril.

"I conclude death does not occur without some premonition. Tell me something more. What precedes death?" inquired Flaxman Low.

"A regular and well-marked series of events—I insist upon calling them events," replied Yarkindale. "This is not a disease with a sequence of symptoms. Whatever it is, it comes from the outside. First, we fall into an indescribable depression, causeless except as being the beginning of the end, for we are all healthy men, fairly rich, and even lucky in the other affairs of life—and of love. Next comes the ghost or apparition, or whatever you like to call it. Lastly, we die by our own hands." Yarkindale brought down a sinewy brown hand upon the arm of his chair. "And because we have been powers in the land, and there must be as little scandal as possible, the doctors and the coroner's jury bring it in 'Temporary insanity.'"

"How long does this depression last before the end?" Flaxman Low's voice broke in upon the other's moody thinking.

"That varies, but the conclusion never. I am the last of the lot, and though I am full of life and health and resolve to-day, I don't give myself a week to live. It is ghastly! To kill oneself is bad enough, but to know that one is being driven to do it, to know that no power on earth can save one, is an outlook of which words can't give the colour."

"But you have not yet seen the apparition—which is the second stage."

"It will come to-day or to-morrow—as soon as I go back to Sevens Hall. I have watched two others of my family go through the same mill. This irresistible depression always comes first. I tell you, in two weeks I shall be dead. And the thought is maddening me!

"I have a wife and child," he went on, after an interval, "and to think of the poor little beggar growing up only to suffer this!"

"Where are they?" asked Low.

"I left them in Florence. I hope the truth can be kept from my wife; but that also is too much to hope. 'Another suicide at Sevens Hall.' I can see the headlines. Those rags of newspapers would sell their mothers for half a crown!"

"Then the other deaths took place at Sevens Hall?"

"All of them." He stopped and looked hard at Mr. Low.

"Tell me about your brothers," said Low.

Yarkindale burst into laughter.

"Well done, Mr. Low! Why didn't you advise me not to go back to Sevens Hall? That is the admirable counsel which the two brain specialists, whom I have seen since I came up to town, have given me. Go back to the Hall? Of course I shouldn't—if I could help it. That's the difficulty—I can't help it! I must go. They thought me mad!"

"I hardly wonder," said Mr. Low calmly, "if you exhibited the same excitement. Now, hear me. If, as you wish me to suppose, you are fighting against supernatural powers, the very first point is to keep a firm and calm control of your feelings and thoughts. It is possible that you and I together may be able to meet this trouble of yours in some new and possibly successful way. Tell me all you can remember with regard to the deaths of your brothers."

"You are right," said Yarkindale sadly enough. "I am behaving like a maniac, and yet I'm sane, Heaven knows! To begin with, there were three of us, and we made up our minds long ago, when we were kids, to see each other through to the last, and we determined not to yield to the influence without a good fight for it. Five years ago my eldest brother went to Somaliland on a shooting trip. He was a big, vigorous, self-willed man, and I was not anxious about him. My second brother, Jack, was an R.E., a clever, sensitive, quiet fellow, more likely to be affected by the tradition of the family. While he was out in Gib., Vane suddenly returned from Africa. I found him changed. He had become gloomy and abstracted, and kept saying that the curse was coming upon him. He insisted upon going down to Sevens Hall. I was savage with him. I thought he should have resisted the inclination; I know more about it now. One night he rushed into my bedroom, crying out: 'He's come; he's come!'"

"Did he ever describe what he had seen?" asked Low.

"Never. None of us know definitely what shape the cursed thing takes. No one of us has ever seen it; or, at any rate, in time to describe it. But once it comes—and this is the horrible part—it never leaves us. Step by step it dogs us, till——" Yarkindale stopped, and in a minute or two resumed. "For two nights I sat up with him. He said very little, for Vane never talked much; but I saw the agony in his face, the fear, the loathing, the growing horror—he who, I believe, had never before feared anything in his life.

"The third night I fell asleep. I was worn out, though I don't offer that as an excuse. I am a light sleeper, yet while I slept Vane killed himself within six feet of me! At the inquest it was proved that he had bought a silken waist-rope at Cairo, and it was contended that he must have concealed it from me, as I had never seen it. I found him with his head nearly twisted off, and a red rubbed weal across his face. He was lying in a heap upon the floor, for the rope was frayed and broken by his struggles. The theory was that he had hanged himself, and then repented of it, and, in his efforts to get free, had wrenched his head round, and scarred his face."

Yarkindale stopped, and shuddered violently.

"I tried to hush the matter up as well as I could, but of course the news of it reached Jack. Then a couple of years passed, and he went from Gib. to India, and wrote in splendid spirits, for he had met a girl he liked out there, and he told me there was never so happy a man on earth before. So you can fancy how I felt when I had a wire from the Hall imploring me to go down at once, for Jack had arrived. It is very hard to tell you what he suffered." Yarkindale broke off and wiped his forehead. "For I have been through it all within the last two weeks myself. He cared for that girl beyond anything on earth; yet within a couple of days of their marriage he had felt himself impelled to rush home to England without so much as bidding her good-bye, though he knew that at the end of his journey death was waiting for him. We talked it over rationally, Mr. Low, and we determined to combine against the power, whatever it was, that was driving him out of the world. We are not monomaniacs. We want to live; we have all that makes life worth living; and yet I am going the same way, and not any effort or desire or resolution on my part can save me!"

"It is a pity you make up your mind to that," said Flaxman Low. "One will pitted against another will has at least a chance of success. And a second point I beg you will bear in mind. Good is always inherently stronger than evil. If, for instance, health were not, broadly speaking, stronger than disease, the poisonous germs floating about the world would kill off the human race inside twelve months."

"Yes," said Yarkindale; "but where two of us failed before, it is not likely that I alone will succeed."

"You need not be alone," said Flaxman Low; "for, if you have no objection, I should be glad to accompany you to Sevens Hall, and to give you any aid that may be in my power."

It is not necessary to record what Yarkindale had to say in answer to this offer. Presently he resumed his story—

"Jack was dispirited, and, unlike Vane, desperately afraid of his fate. He hardly dared to fall asleep. He recalled all he knew of our father's death, and tried to draw me on to describe Vane's, but I knew better than that. Still, with all my care, he went the same way! I did not trust my own watchfulness a second time; I had a man in the house who was a trained attendant. He sat outside Jack's door of nights. One morning early—it was summertime, and he must have dropped into a doze—he was shoved over, chair and all, and before he could pick himself up Jack had flung himself from the balcony outside one of the gallery windows."

Sevens Hall is a large Elizabethan mansion hidden away among acres of rich pasture-lands, where wild-flowers bloom abundantly in their seasons, and rooks build and caw in the great elms. But none of the natural beauties of the country were visible when Mr. Low arrived late on a November evening with Yarkindale. The interior of the house, however, made up for the bleakness outside.

Fires and lights blazed in the hall and in the principal rooms.

During dinner, Yarkindale seemed to have relapsed into his most dejected mood. He scarcely opened his lips, and his face looked black, not only with depression, but anger. For he was by no means ready to give up life; he rebelled against his fate with the strenuous fury of a man whose pride and strength of will and nearest desires are baffled by an antagonist he cannot evade.

During the evening they played billiards, for Low was aware that the less his companion thought over his own position the better.

Flaxman Low arranged to occupy a room opposite Yarkindale's. So far the latter was in the same state as on the day when first he saw Mr. Low. He was conscious of the same deep and causeless depression, and the wish to return to Sevens Hall had grown beyond his power to resist. But the second of the fatal signs, the following footsteps, had not yet been heard.

During the next forenoon, to Yarkindale's surprise, Flaxman Low, instead of avoiding the subject, threshed out the details of the former deaths at Sevens Hall, especially those of which Yarkindale could give the fullest particulars. He examined the balcony from which Jack Yarkindale had thrown himself. The ironwork was wrenched and broken in one part.

"When did this happen?" asked Low, pointing to it.

"On the night that Jack died," was the reply. "I have been very little at home since, and I did not care at the time to bother about having it put right."

"It looks," said Flaxman Low, "as if he had had a struggle for his life, and clung to the upper bar here where it is bent outwards. He had wounds on his hands, had he not?" he continued, looking at a dull long splash of rust upon the iron.

"Yes, his hands were bleeding."

"Please try to recollect exactly. Were they cut or bruised upon the palm? Or was it on the back?"

"Now I come to think of it, his hands were a good deal injured, especially on the knuckles—one wrist was broken—by the fall no doubt."

Flaxman Low made no remark.

Next they went into the spacious bedroom where Vane and more than one of those who went before him had died, and which Yarkindale now occupied. His companion asked to see the rope with which Vane had hanged himself. Most unwillingly Yarkindale brought it out. The two pieces, with their broken strands and brown stains, appeared to be of great interest to Low. He next saw the exact spot on the great bedstead from which it had been suspended, and searching along the back, he discovered the jagged edge of wood against which Vane in his last agony had endeavoured to free himself by fraying the rope.

"We suppose the rope gave after he was dead, and that was because of his great weight," said Yarkindale. "This is the room in which most of the tragedies have taken place. You will probably witness the last one."

"That will depend on yourself," answered Flaxman Low. "I am inclined to think there will be no tragedy if you will stiffen your back, and hold out. Did either of your brothers on waking complain of dreams?"

Yarkindale looked suspiciously at him from under drawn brows. "Yes," he said harshly, "they both spoke of tormenting dreams, which they could not recall after waking, but that also was taken as a symptom of brain disease by the experts. And now that you have learned more about the matter, you, too, begin upon the old, worn theory."

"On the contrary, my theory has nothing whatever to do with insanity, though the phenomena connected with the deaths of your brothers seem to be closely associated with sleep. You tell me your brother Jack was afraid to sleep. Your other brother awoke to find his death somehow. Therefore, we may be certain that at a certain stage of these series of events, as you call them, sleep becomes both a dread and a danger."

Yarkindale shivered and glanced nervously over his shoulder.

"This room is growing very cold. Let us go down to the hall. As for sleep, I have been afraid of it for a long time."

All the day Low noticed that his companion continued to look excessively pale and nervous. Every now and then he would turn his face round as if listening. In the evening they again played billiards late into the night. The house was full of silence before they went upstairs. A long strip of polished flooring led from the billiard-room door to the hall. Yarkindale motioned to Low to stand still while he walked slowly to the foot of the staircase. In the stillness Flaxman Low distinctly heard mingled steps, a softer tread following upon Yarkindale's purposely loud footfalls. The hall was in darkness with the exception of a gas-jet at the staircase. Yarkindale stopped, leant heavily against the pillar of the balustrade, and with a ghastly face waited for Low to join him. Then he gripped Low by the arm and pointed downwards. Beside his shadow a second dim, hooded, formless shadow showed faintly on the floor.

"Stage two," said Yarkindale. "You see it is no fancy of our unhealthy brains."

Mr. Low has placed it upon record that the following week contained one of the most painful experiences through which it has been his lot to pass. Yarkindale fought doggedly for his life. He thrust aside his dejection. He followed the advice given him with marvellous courage. But still the ominous days dragged on, seeming at times too slow, at times too rapid in their passage. Yarkindale's physical strength began to fail—a mental battle is the most exhausting of all struggles.

"The next point in which you can help," said Low on the eighth night, "is to try to recollect what you have been dreaming of immediately before waking."

Yarkindale shook his head despondently.

"I have tried over and over again, and though I wake in a cold sweat of terror, I cannot gather my senses quickly enough to seize the remembrance of the thing that has spoiled my sleep," he answered, with a pallid smile. "You think the psychological moment with us is undoubtedly the first waking moment?"

Low admitted that he thought it was so.

"I understand now why you have emptied this room of everything except the two couches on which we lie. You are afraid I shall lay hands upon myself! I feel the danger, and yet I have no suicidal desire. I want to live—Heaven, how long to live! To be happy, and prosperous, and light-hearted, as I once was!"

Yarkindale lay back upon the couch.

"I wish I could give you the faintest notion of the desperate misery in my mind to-night! I could almost ask to die to escape from it!" he went on; "the burden only appears to grow heavier and more unbearable every day—I sometimes feel I can no longer endure it."

"Think, on the contrary, how much you have to live for. For your own self it matters less than for your boy. Your victory may mean his."

"How? Tell me how?"

"It is rather a long explanation, and I think we had better defer it until I can form some rather more definite ideas on the subject."

"Very well." Yarkindale turned his face from the light. "I will try to sleep, and forget all this wretchedness if I can. You will not leave me?"

Throughout the long winter night Flaxman Low watched beside him. He felt he dared not leave him for one moment. The room was almost dark, for Yarkindale could not sleep otherwise. The flickering firelight died slowly down, until nothing was left of the last layer of glowing wood ashes. The night lamp in a distant corner threw long shadows across the empty floor, that wavered now and then as if a wind touched the flame.

Outside, the night was still and black; not a sound disturbed the silence except those strange unaccountable creakings and groanings which seem like inarticulate voices in an old house.

Yarkindale was sleeping heavily, and as the night deepened Low got up and walked about the room in circles, always keeping his face towards the sleeper. The air had grown very cold, and when he sat down again he drew a rug about him, and lit a cigar. The change in the atmosphere was sudden and peculiar, and he softly pulled his couch close to Yarkindale's and waited.

Creakings and groanings floated up and down the gaunt old corridors; the mystery and loneliness of night became oppressive. The shadow from the night-lamp swayed and fluttered as if a door had been opened. Mr. Low glanced at both doors. He had locked both, and both were closed, yet the flame bent and fluttered until Low put his hand across his companion's chest, so that he might at once detect any waking movement, for the light had now become too dim to see by.

To his intense surprise he found his hand at once in the chill of a cold draught blowing upon it from above. But Flaxman Low had no time to think about it, for a horrible feeling of cold and numbness was also stealing upwards through his feet, and a sense of weight and deadly chill seemed pressing in upon his shoulders and back. The back of his neck ached, his outstretched hand began to stiffen.

Yarkindale still slept heavily.

New sensations were borne in slowly upon Low. The chill around him was repulsive and clammy. Desperate desires awoke in his mind; something that could almost be felt was beating down his will.

Then Yarkindale moved slightly in his sleep.

Low was conscious of a supreme struggle, whether of mind or body he does not know, but to him it appeared to extend to the ultimate effort a man can make. A hideous temptation rushed wildly across his thoughts to murder Yarkindale! A dreadful longing to feel the man's strong throat yielding and crushing under his own sinewy strangling fingers, was forced into his mind.

Suddenly, Low became aware that, although the couch and part of Yarkindale's figure were visible, his head and the upper part of the body were blotted out as if by some black intervening object. But there was no outline of the interposed form, nothing but a vague, thick blackness.

He sprang to his feet as he heard an ominous choking gasp from Yarkindale, and with swift hands he felt over the body through the darkness. Yarkindale lay tense and stiff.

"Yarkindale!" shouted Low, as his fingers felt the angle of an elbow, then hands upon Yarkindale's throat, hands that clutched savagely with fingers of iron.

"Wake, man!" shouted Low again, trying to loosen the desperate clutch. Then he knew that the hands were Yarkindale's own hands, and that the man was apparently strangling himself.

The ghastly struggle that, in the darkness, seemed half a dream and half reality, ceased abruptly when Yarkindale moved, and his hands fell limp and slack into Low's as the darkness between them cleared away.

"Are you awake?" Low called again.

"Yes. What is it? I feel as if I had been fighting for my life. Or have I been very ill?"

"Both, in a sense. But the worst is over. Hold on, the lamp's gone out."

But, as he spoke, the light resumed its steady glimmer, and, when a couple of candles added their brightness, the room was shown bare and empty, and as securely closed as ever. The only change to be noted was that the temperature had risen.

*

A frosty sun was shining into the library windows next morning when Flaxman Low talked out the matter of the haunting presence which had exerted so sinister an influence upon generations of the Yarkindale family.

"Before you say anything, I wish to admit, Mr. Low, that I, and no doubt those who have gone before me, have certainly suffered from a transient touch of suicidal mania," began Yarkindale gloomily.

"And I am very sure you make a mistake," replied Low. "In suicidal mania the idea is not transient, but persistent, often extending over months, during which time the patient watches for an opportunity to make away with himself. In your own case, when I woke you last night, you were aware of a desire to strangle yourself, but directly you became thoroughly awake the idea left you?"

"That is so. Still——"

"You know that often when dreaming one imagines oneself to do many things which in the waking state would be entirely impossible, yet one continues subject to the idea for a moment or so during the intermittent stage between waking and sleeping. If one has a nightmare, one continues to feel a beating of the heart and a sensation of fright even for some interval after waking. Yours was an analogous condition."

"But look here, Mr. Low. How do you account for it that I, who at this moment have not the slightest desire to make away with myself, should, at the moment of awaking from sleep, be driven to doing precisely that which I detest and wish to avoid?"

"In every particular," said Flaxman Low, "your brothers' cases were similar. Each of them attempted his life in that transient moment while the will and reason were still passive, and action was still subject to an abnormally vivid idea which had evidently been impressed upon the consciousness during sleep. We have clear proof of this, I say, in the struggles of each to save himself when actually *in extremis*. Contemporary psychology has arrived at the conclusion that every man possesses a subconscious as well as a conscious self," added Low, after a pause. "This second or submerged self appears to be infinitely more susceptible of spiritual influences than the conscious personality. Such influences work most strongly when the normal self is in abeyance during sleep, dreaming, or the hypnotic condition. In your own family you have an excellent example of the idea of self-destruction being suggested during sleep, and carried into action during the first confused, unmastered moments of waking."

"But how do you account for the following footsteps? Whose wishes or suggestions do we obey?"

"I believe them to be different manifestations of the same evil intelligence. Ghosts sometimes, as possibly you are aware, pursue a purpose, and your family has been held in subjection by a malicious spirit that has goaded them on to destroy themselves. I could bring forward a number of other examples; there is the Black Friar of the Sinclairs and the Fox of the Oxenholms. To come back to your own case—do you remember of what you dreamed before I woke you?"

Yarkindale looked troubled.

"I have a dim recollection, but it eludes me. I cannot fix it." He glanced round the room, as if searching for a reminder. Suddenly he sprang up and approached a picture on the wall—"Here it is!" he shouted. "I remember now. A dark figure stood over me; I saw the long face and the sinister eyes; it was this man—Jules Cevaine!"

"You have not spoken of Cevaine before. Who was he?"

"He was the last of the old Cevaines. You know this house is called Sevens Hall—a popular corruption of the Norman name Cevaine. We Yarkindales were distant cousins, and inherited this place after the death of Jules Cevaine, about a hundred years ago. He was said to have taken a prominent part—under another name—in the Reign of Terror. However that may be—he resented our inheriting the Hall."

"He died here?" asked Flaxman Low.

"Yes."

"His purpose in haunting you," said Low, "was doubtless the extermination of your family. His spirit lingers about this spot where the final intense passion of terror, pain, and hatred was felt. And you yourselves have unknowingly fostered his power by dwelling upon and dreading his influence, thus opening the way to spirit communication, until from time to time his disembodied will has superimposed itself upon your wills during the bewildered moment of waking, and the several successive tragedies of which you told me have been the result."

"Then how can we ever escape?"

"You have already won one and your most important victory; for the rest, think of him as seldom as may be. Destroy this painting, and any other articles that may have belonged to him; and if you take my advice you will travel for a while."

In pursuance of Mr. Flaxman Low's advice, Yarkindale went for the cold weather to India. He has had no recurrence of the old trouble, but he loathes Sevens Hall, and he is only waiting for his son to be old enough to break the entail, when the property will be placed on the market.

THE STORY OF SADDLER'S CROFT

Although Flaxman Low has devoted his life to the study of psychical phenomena, he has always been most earnest in warning persons who feel inclined to dabble in spiritualism, without any serious motive for doing so, of the mischief and danger accruing to the rash experimenter. Extremely few persons are sufficiently masters of themselves to permit of their calling in the vast unknown forces outside ordinary human knowledge for mere purposes of amusement.

In support of this warning the following extraordinary story is laid before our readers.

*

Deep in the forest land of Sussex, close by an unfrequented road, stands a low half-timbered house, that is only separated from the roadway by a rough stone wall and a few flower borders. The front is covered with ivy, and looks out between two conical trees upon the passers-by. The windows are many of them diamond-paned, and an unpretentious white gate leads up to the front door. It is a quaint, quiet spot, with an old-world suggestion about it which appealed strongly to pretty Sadie Corcoran as she drove with her husband along the lane. The Corcorans were Americans, and had to the full the American liking for things ancient. Saddler's Croft struck them both as ideal, and when they found out that it was much more roomy and comfortable than it looked from the road, and also that it had large lawns and grounds attached to it, they decided at once on taking it for a year or two.

When they mentioned the project to Phil Strewd, their host, and an old friend of Corcoran, he did not favour it. Much as he should have liked to have them for neighbours, he thought that Saddler's Croft had too many unpleasant traditions connected with it. Besides, it had lain empty for three years, as the last occupants were spiritualists of some sort, and the place was said to be haunted. But Mrs. Corcoran was not to be put off, and declared that a flavour of ghostliness was all that Saddler's Croft required to make it absolutely the most attractive residence in Europe.

The Corcorans moved in about October, but it was not till the following July that Flaxman Low met Mr. Strewd on the Victoria platform.

"I'm glad you're coming down to Andy Corcoran's," Strewd began. "You must remember him? I introduced you to him at the club a couple of years ago. He's an awfully decent fellow, and an old friend of mine. He once went with an Arctic expedition, and has crossed Greenland or San Josef's Land on snowshoes or something. I've got the book about it at home. So you can size him up for yourself. He's now married to a very pretty woman, and they have taken a house in my part of the world.

"I didn't want them to rent Saddler's Croft, for it had a bad name some years ago. Some of your psychical folk used to live there. They made a sort of Greek temple at the back, where they used to have queer goings on, so I'm told. A Greek was living with them called Agapoulos, who was the arch-priest of their sect, or whatever it was. Ultimately Agapoulos died on a moonlight night in the temple, in the middle of their rites. After that his friends left, but, of course, people said he haunted the place. I never saw anything myself, but a young sailor, home on leave about that time, swore he'd catch the ghost, and he was found next morning on the temple steps. He was past telling us what had happened, or what he had seen, for he was dead. I'll never forget his face. It was horrible!"

"And since then?"

"After that the place would not let, although the talk of the ghost being seen died away until quite lately. I suppose the old caretaker went to bed early, and avoided trouble that way. But during the last few months Corcoran has seen it repeatedly himself, and—in fact, things seem to be going on very strangely. What with Mrs. Corcoran wild on studying psychology, as she calls it——"

"So Mrs. Corcoran has a turn that way?"

"Yes, since young Sinclair came home from Ceylon about five months ago. I must tell you he was very thick with Agapoulos in former times, and people said he used to join in all the ruffianism at Saddler's Croft. You'll see the rest for yourself. You are asked down ostensibly to please Mrs. Corcoran, but Andy hopes you may help him to clear up the mystery."

Flaxman Low found Corcoran a tall, thin, nervy American of the best type; while his wife was as pretty and as charming as we have grown accustomed to expect an American girl to be.

"I suppose," Corcoran began, "that Phil has been giving you all the gossip about this house? I was entirely sceptical once; but now—do you believe in midsummer madness?"

"I believe there often is a deep truth hidden in common beliefs and superstitions. But let me hear more."

"I'll tell you what happened not twenty-four hours ago. Everything has been working up to it for the last three months, but it came to a head last night, and I immediately wired for you. I had been sitting in my smoking-room rather late reading. I put out the lamp and was just about to go to bed when the brilliance of the moonlight struck me, and I put my head through the window to look over the lawn. Directly I heard chanting of a most unusual character from the direction of the temple, which lies at the back of that plantation. Then one voice, a beautiful tenor, detached itself from the rest, and seemed to approach the house. As it came nearer I saw my wife cross the grass to the plantation with a wavering, uncertain gait. I ran after her, for I believed she was walking in her sleep; but before I could reach her a man came out of the grass alley at the other side of the lawn.

"I saw them go away together down the alley towards the temple, but I could not stir, the moonbeams seemed to be penetrating my brain, my feet were chained, the wildest and most hideous thoughts seemed rocking—I can use no other term—in my head. I made an effort, and ran round by another way, and met them on the temple steps. I had strength left to grasp at the man—remember I saw him plainly, with his dark, Greek face—but he turned aside and leapt into the underwood, leaving in my hand only the button from the back of his coat.

"Now comes the incomprehensible part. Sadie, without seeing me, or so it appeared, glided away again towards the house; but I was determined to find the man who had eluded me. The moonlight poured upon my head; I felt it like an absolute touch. The chanting grew louder, and drowned every other recollection. I forgot Sadie, I forgot all but the delicious sounds, and I—I, a nineteenth-century, hard-headed Yankee—hammered at those accursed doors to be allowed to enter. Then, like a dream, the singing was behind me and around me—some one came, or so I thought, and pushed me gently in. The moon was pouring through the end window; there were many people. In the morning I found myself lying on the floor of the temple, and all about me the dust was undisturbed but for the mark of my own single footstep and the spot where I had fallen. You may say it was all a dream, Low, but I tell you some infernal power hangs about that building."

"From what you tell me," said Flaxman Low, "I can almost undertake to say that Mrs. Corcoran is at present nearly, if not quite, ignorant of the horrible experience you remember. In her case the emotions of wonder and curiosity have probably alone been worked upon as in a dream."

"I believe in her absolutely," exclaimed Corcoran, "but this power swamps all resistance. I have another strange circumstance to add. On coming to myself I found the button still in my hand. I have since had the opportunity of fitting it to its right position in the coat of a man who is a pretty constant visitor here," the American's lips tightened, "a young Sinclair, who does tea-planting in Ceylon when he has the health for it, but is just now at home to recruit. He is the son of a neighbouring squire, and in every particular of face and figure unlike the handsome Greek I saw that night."

"Have you spoken to him on the subject?"

"Yes; I showed him the button, and told him I had found it near the temple. He took the news very curiously. He did not look confused or guilty, but simply scared out of his senses. He offered no explanation, but made a hasty excuse, and left us. My wife looked on with the most perfect indifference, and offered no remark."

"Has Mrs. Corcoran appeared to be very languid of late?" asked Low.

"Yes, I have noticed that."

"Judging from the effect produced by the chanting upon you, I should say that you were something of a musician?" said Low irrelevantly.

"Yes," replied the other, astonished.

"Then, this evening, when I am talking with Mrs. Corcoran, will you reproduce the melody you heard on that night?"

Corcoran agreed, and the conversation ended with a request on the part of Mr. Low to be permitted to make the acquaintance of Mrs. Corcoran, and further, to be given the opportunity of talking to her alone.

Sadie Corcoran received him with effusion.

"O Mr. Low, I'm just perfectly delighted to see you! I'm looking forward to the most lovely spiritual talks. It's such fun! You know I was in quite a psychical set before I married, but afterwards I dropped it, because Andy has some effete old prejudices."

Flaxman Low inquired how it happened that her interest had revived.

"It is the air of this dear old place," she replied, with a more serious expression. "I always found the subject very attractive, and lately we have made the acquaintance of a Mr. Sinclair, who is a——" she checked herself with an odd look, "who knows all about it."

"How does he advise you to experiment?" asked Mr. Low. "Have you ever tried sleeping with the moonlight on your face?"

She flushed, and looked startled.

"Yes, Mr. Sinclair told me that the spiritualists who formerly lived in this house believed that by doing so you could put yourself into communication with—other intelligences. It makes one dream," she added, "such strange dreams."

"Are they pleasant dreams?" asked Flaxman Low gravely.

"Not now, but by and by he assures me that they will be."

"But you must think of your dreams all day long, or the moonlight will not affect you so readily on the next occasion, and you are obliged to repeat a certain formula? Is it not so?"

She admitted it was, and added: "But Mr. Sinclair says that if I persevere I shall soon pass through the zone of the bad spirits and enter the circle of the good. So I choose to go on. It is all so wonderful and exciting. Oh, here is Mr. Sinclair! I'm sure you will find many interesting things to talk over."

The drawing-room lay at the back of the house, and overlooked a strip of lawn shut in on the further side by a thick plantation of larches. Directly opposite to the French window, where they were seated, a grass alley which had been cut through the plantation gave a glimpse of turf and forest land beyond. From this alley now emerged a young man in riding-breeches, who walked moodily across the lawn with his eyes on the ground. In a few minutes Flaxman Low understood that young Sinclair had a pronounced admiration for his hostess, the reckless, headstrong admiration with which a weak-willed man of strong emotions often deceives himself and the woman he loves. He was manifestly in wretched health and equally wretched spirits, a combination that greatly impaired the very ordinary type of English good-looks which he represented.

While the three had tea together Mrs. Corcoran made some attempt to lead up to the subject of spiritualism, but Sinclair avoided it, and soon Mrs. Corcoran lost her vivacity, which gave place to a well-marked languor, a condition that Low shortly grew to connect with Sinclair's presence. Presently she left them, and the two men went outside and walked up and down smoking for a while till Flaxman Low turned down the path between the larches. Sinclair hung back.

"You'll find it stuffy down there," he said, with curved nostrils.

"I rather wanted to see what building that roof over the trees belongs to," replied Low.

With manifest reluctance Sinclair went on beside him. Another turn at right angles brought them into the path leading up to the little temple, which Low found was solidly built of stone. In shape it was oblong, with a pillared Ionic facade. The trees stood closely round it, and it contained only one window, now void of glass, set high in the further end of the building. Low asked a question.

"It was a summer-house made by the people who lived here formerly," replied Sinclair, with brusqueness. "Let's get away. It's beastly damp."

"It is an odd kind of summer-house. It looks more like——" Low checked himself. "Can we go inside?" He went up the low steps and tried the door, which yielded readily, and he entered to look round.

The walls had once been ornamented with designs in black and some glittering pigment, while at the upper end a daïs nearly four feet high stood under the arched window, the whole giving the vague impression of a church. One or two peculiarities of structure and decoration struck Low. He turned sharply on Sinclair.

"What was this place used for?"

But Sinclair was staring round with a white, working face; his glance seemed to trace out the half-obliterated devices upon the walls, and then rested on the daïs. A sort of convulsion passed over his features, as his head was jerked forward, rather as if pushed by some unseen force than by his own will, while, at the same time, he brought his hand to his mouth, and kissed it. Then with a strange, prolonged cry he rushed headlong out of the temple, and appeared no more at Saddler's Croft that day.

The afternoon was still and warm with brooding thunderstorm, but at night the sky cleared. Now it happened that Andy Corcoran was, amongst many other good things, an accomplished musician, and, while Flaxman Low and Mrs. Corcoran talked at intervals by the open French window, he sat down at the piano and played a weird melody. Mrs. Corcoran broke off in the middle of a sentence, and soon she began swaying gently to the rhythm of the music, and presently she was singing. Suddenly, Corcoran dropped his hand on the notes with a crash. His wife sprang from her chair.

"Andy! Where are you? Where are you?" And in a moment she had thrown herself, sobbing hysterically, into his arms, while he begged her to tell him what troubled her.

"It was that music. Oh, don't play it any more! I liked it at first, and then all at once it seemed to terrify me!" He led her back towards the light.

"Where did you learn that song, Sadie? Tell me."

She lifted her clear eyes to his.

"I don't know! I can't remember, but it is like a dreadful memory! Never play it again! Promise me!"

"Of course not, darling."

*

By midnight the moon sailed broad and bright above the house. Flaxman Low and the American were together in the smoking-room. The room was in darkness. Low sat in the shadow of the open window, while Corcoran waited behind him in the gloom. The shade of the larches lay in a black line along the grass, the air was still and heavy, not a leaf moved. From his position, Low could see the dark masses of the forest stretching away into the dimness over the undulating country. The scene was very lovely, very lonely, and very sad.

A little trill of bells within the room rang the half-hour after midnight, and scarcely had the sound ceased when from outside came another—a long cadenced wailing chant of voices in unison that rose and fell faint and far off but with one distinct note, the same that Low had heard in Sinclair's beast-like cry earlier in the day.

After the chanting died away, there followed a long sullen interval, broken at last by a sound of singing, but so vague and dim that it might have been some elusive air throbbing within the brain. Slowly it grew louder and nearer. It was the melody Sadie had begged never to hear again, and it was sung by a tenor voice, vibrating and beautiful.

Low felt Corcoran's hand grip his shoulder, when out upon the grass Sadie, a slim figure in trailing white, appeared advancing with uncertain steps towards the alley of the larches. The next moment the singer came forward from the shadows to meet her. It was not Sinclair, but a much more remarkable-looking personage. He stopped and raised his face to the moon, a face of an extraordinary perfection of beauty such as Flaxman Low had never seen before. But the great dark eyes, the full powerfully moulded features, had one attribute in common with Sinclair's face, they wore the same look of a profound and infinite unhappiness.

"Come." Corcoran gripped Flaxman Low's shoulder. "She is sleep-walking. We will see who it is this time."

When they reached the lawn the couple had disappeared. Corcoran leading, the two men ran along under the shadow of the house, and so by another path to the back of the temple.

The empty window glowed in the light of the moon, and the hum of a subdued chanting floated out amongst the silent trees. The sound seized upon the brain like a whiff of opium, and a thousand unbidden thoughts ran through Flaxman Low's mind. But his mental condition was as much under his control as his bodily movements. Pulling himself together he ran on. Sadie Corcoran and her companion were mounting the steps under the pillars. The girl held back, as if drawn forward against her will; her eyes were blank and open, and she moved slowly.

Then Corcoran dashed out of the shadow.

What occurred next Mr. Low does not know, for he hurried Mrs. Corcoran away towards the house, holding her arm gently. She yielded to his touch, and went silently beside him to the drawing-room, where he guided her to a couch. She lay down upon it like a tired child, and closed her eyes without a word.

After a while Flaxman Low went out again to look for Corcoran. The temple was dark and silent, and there was no one to be seen. He groped his way through the long grass towards the back of the building. He had not gone far when he stumbled over something soft that moved and groaned. Low lit a match, for it was impossible to see anything in the gloom under the trees. To his horror he found the American at his feet, beaten and battered almost beyond recognition.

The first thing next morning Mr. Strewd received a note from Flaxman Low asking him to come over at once. He arrived in the course of the forenoon, and listened to an account of Corcoran's adventures during the night, with an air of dismay.

"So it's come at last!" he remarked, "I'd no idea Sinclair was such a bruiser."

"Sinclair? What do you suppose Sinclair had to do with it?"

"Oh, come now, Low, what's the good of that? Why, my man told me this morning when I was shaving that Sinclair went home some time last night all over blood. I'd half a guess at what had happened then."

"But I tell you I saw the man with whom Corcoran fought. He was an extraordinarily handsome man with a Greek face."

Strewd whistled.

"By George, Low, you let your imagination run away with you," he said, shaking his head. "That's all nonsense, you know."

"We must try to find out if it is," said Low.

"Will you come over to-night and stay with me? There will be a full moon."

"Yes, and it has affected all your brains! Here's Mrs. Corcoran full of surprise over her husband's condition! You don't suppose that's genuine?"

"I know it is genuine," replied Low quietly. "Bring your Kodak with you when you come, will you?"

The day was long, languorous, and heavy; the thunderstorm had not yet broken, but once again the night rose cloudless. Flaxman Low decided to watch alone near the temple while Strewd remained on the alert in the house, ready to give his help if it should be needed.

The hush of the night, the smell of the dewy larches, the silvery light with its bewildering beauty creeping from point to point as the moon rose, all the pure influences of nature, seemed to Low more powerful, more effective, than he had ever before felt them to be. Forcing his mind to dwell on ordinary subjects, he waited. Midnight passed, and then began indistinct sounds, shuffling footsteps, murmurings, and laughter, but all faint and evasive. Gradually the tumultuous thoughts he had experienced on the previous evening began to run riot in his brain.

When the singing began he does not know. It was only by an immense effort of will that he was able to throw off the trance that was stealing over him, holding him prisoner—how nearly a willing prisoner he shudders to remember. But habits of self-control have been Low's only shield in many a dangerous hour. They came to his aid now. He moved out in front of the temple just in time to see Sadie pass within the temple door. Waiting only a moment to make quite sure of his senses, and concentrating his will on the single desire of saving her, he followed. He says he was conscious of a crowd of persons at either side; he knew without looking that the pictures on the wall glowed and lived again.

Through the high window opposite him a broad white shaft of light fell, and immediately under it, on the daïs, stood the man whom Mr. Low in his heart now called Agapoulos. Supreme in its beauty and its sadness that beautiful face looked across the bowed heads of those present into the eyes of Mr. Flaxman Low. Slowly, very slowly, as a narrow lane opened up before him amongst the figures of the crowd, Low advanced towards the daïs. The man's smile seemed to draw him on; he stretched out his hand as Flaxman Low approached. And Low was conscious of a longing to clasp it even though that might mean perdition.

At the last moment, when it seemed to him he could resist no longer, he became aware of the white-clad figure of Sadie beside him. She also was looking up at the beautiful face with a wild gaze. Low hesitated no longer. He was now within two feet of the daïs. He swung back his left hand and dealt a smashing half-arm blow at the figure. The man staggered with a very human groan, and then fell face forward on the daïs. A whirlwind of dust seemed to rise and obscure the moonlight; there was a wild sense of motion and flight, a subdued sibilant murmur like the noise of a swarm of bats in commotion, and then Flaxman Low heard Phil Strewd's loud voice at the door, and he shouted to him to come.

"What has happened?" said Strewd, as he helped to raise the fallen man. "Why, whom have we got here? Good heavens, Low, it is Agapoulos! I remember him well!"

"Leave him there in the moonlight. Take Mrs. Corcoran away and hurry back with the Kodak. There is no time to lose before the moon leaves this window."

The moonlight was full and strong, the exposure prolonged and steady, so that when afterwards Flaxman Low came to develop the film—but we are anticipating, for the night and its revelations were not over yet. The two men waited through the dark hour that precedes the dawn, intending when daylight came to remove their prisoner elsewhere. They sat on the edge of the daïs side by side, Strewd at Low's request holding the hand of the unconscious man, and talked till the light came.

"I think it's about time to move him now," suggested Strewd, looking round at the wounded man behind him. As he did so, he sprang to his feet with a shout.

"What's this, Low? I've gone mad, I think! Look here!"

Flaxman Low bent over the pale, unconscious face. It bore no longer the impress of that exquisite Greek beauty they had seen an hour earlier; it only showed to their astonished gaze the haggard outlines of young Sinclair.

*

Some days later Strewd rubbed the back of his head energetically with a broad hand, and surmised aloud.

"This is a strange world, my masters," and he looked across the cool shady bedroom at Andy Corcoran's bandaged head.

"And the other world's stranger, I guess," put in the American drily, "if we may judge by the sample of the supernatural we have lately had."

"You know I hold that there is no such thing as the supernatural; all is natural," said Flaxman Low. "We need more light, more knowledge. As there is a well-defined break in the notes of the human voice, so there is a break between what we call natural and supernatural. But the notes of the upper register correspond with those in the lower scale; in like manner, by drawing upon our experience of things we know and see, we should be able to form accurate hypotheses with regard to things which, while clearly pertaining to us, have so far been regarded as mysteries."

"I doubt if any theory will touch this mystery," Strewd objected. "I have questioned Sinclair, and noted down his answers as you asked me, Low. Here they are."

"No, thank you. Will you compare my theory with what he has told you? In the first place, Agapoulos was, I fancy, one of a clique calling themselves Dianists, who desired to revive the ancient worship of the moon. That I easily gathered from the symbol of the moon in front of the temple and from the half-defaced devices on the walls inside. Then I perceived that Sinclair, when we were standing before the daïs, almost unconsciously used the gesture of the moon worshippers. The chant we heard was the lament for Adonis. I could multiply evidences, but there is no need to do so. The fact also tells that the place is haunted on moonlight nights only."

"Sinclair's confession corroborates all this," said Strewd at this point.

Corcoran turned irritably on his couch.

"Moon-worship was not exactly the nicest form of idolatry," he said in a weary tone; "but I can't see how that accounts for the awkward fact that a man who not only looks like Agapoulos, but was caught, and even photographed as Agapoulos, turns out at the end of an hour or so, during which there was no chance of substituting one for the other, to be another person of an entirely different appearance. Add to this that Agapoulos is dead and Sinclair is living, and we have an array of facts that drive one to suspect that common-sense and reason are delusions. Go on, Low."

"The substitution, as you call it, of Agapoulos for Sinclair is one of the most marked and best attested cases of obsession with which I have personally come into contact," answered Flaxman Low. "You will notice that during Sinclair's absence in Ceylon nothing was seen of the ghost—on his return it again appeared."

"What is obsession? I know what it is supposed to be, but——" Corcoran stopped.

"I should call it in this case as nearly as possible an instance of spiritual hypnotism. We know there is such a thing as human hypnotism; why should not a disembodied spirit have similar powers? Sinclair has been obsessed by the spirit of Agapoulos; he not only yielded to his influence in the man's lifetime, but sought it again after his death. I don't profess to claim any great knowledge of the subject, but I do know that terrible results have come about from similar practices. Sinclair, for his own reasons, invited the control of a spirit, and, having no inherent powers of resistance, he became its slave. Agapoulos must have possessed extraordinary will-force; his soul actually dominated Sinclair's. Thus not only the mental attributes of Sinclair but even his bodily appearance became modified to the likeness of the Greek. Sinclair himself probably looked upon his experiences as a series of vivid dreams induced by dwelling on certain thoughts and using certain formulæ, until this morning when his condition proved to him that they were real enough."

"That is perhaps all very well so far as it goes," put in Strewd, "but I fail to understand how a seedy, weakly chap like Sinclair could punish my friend Andy here, as we must suppose he has done, if we accept your ideas, Low."

"You are aware that under abnormal conditions, such as may be observed in the insane, a quite extraordinary reserve of latent strength is frequently called out from apparently weak persons. So Sinclair's usual powers were largely reinforced by abnormal influences."

"I have another question to ask, Low," said Corcoran. "Can you explain the strange attraction and influence the temple possessed over all of us, and especially over my wife?"

"I think so. Mrs. Corcoran, through a desire for amusement and excitement, placed herself in a degree of communication with the spiritual world during sleep. Remember, the Greek lived here, and the thoughts and emotions of individuals remain in the *aura* of places closely associated with them. Personally, I do not doubt that Agapoulos is a strong and living intelligence, and those persons who frequent the vicinity of the temple are readily placed in rapport with his wandering spirit by means of this *aura*. To use common words, evil influences haunt the temple."

"But this is intolerable. What can we do?"

"Leave Saddler's Croft, and persuade Mrs. Corcoran to have no more to do with spiritism. As for Sinclair, I will see him. He has opened what may be called the doors of life. It will be a hard task to close them again, and to become his own master. But it may be done."

THE STORY OF № 1 KARMA CRESCENT

The following story is the first full relation of the extraordinary features of the case connected with the house in South London that at one time occupied so large a portion of the public attention. It may be remembered that several mysterious deaths took place within a few months of each other in a certain new suburb. In each instance the same unaccountable symptoms were present, and the successive inquests gave rise to a quite remarkable amount of discussion in the press, as the evidence furnished points of peculiar interest to the Psychical Societies.

It is a recognised fact that the public will die patiently, and to a large percentage, of any known and preventable epidemic before they trouble to make a stir about it; but they resent instantly and bitterly the removal of half a dozen individuals, provided these die from some unknown and, therefore, unpreventable cause. Thus the fate of the victims at № 1 Karma Crescent raised a storm of comment, conjecture, and vague accusation; in time this died away, however, and the whole business was forgotten, or only recalled to serve as an example of the many dark and sinister mysteries London carries in her unfathomed heart.

As many people may not be able to recall the details to mind, a brief *résumé* of the chief incidents is given below, together with additional information supplied later by Flaxman Low, the well-known psychical investigator.

Karma Crescent is one of several similar terraces planned and partially built upon a newly-opened estate in an outlying suburb of London. The locality is good, though not fashionable, hence the houses, though of fair size, are offered at moderate rentals. Karma Crescent has never been completed. It consists of six or seven houses, most of which were let when Colonel Simpson B. Hendriks and his son walked over from the railway station to inspect № 1. This was a detached corner house, overlooking an untidy spread of building-ground, beyond which railway sheds and a network of lines on a rather high level rose against the sky. To the right of the house an old country lane, deeply rutted, led away between ragged hedges to a congeries of small houses about half a mile distant. These houses form the outer crust of a poor district, about which no more need be said than that it provides a certain amount of dock labour.

The Americans were, however, not deterred by the dreary surroundings; they had come to London on business, and since № 1 was cheap, commodious, and well-furnished, they closed with the agent who showed them over the house. It was only when the lease was signed, and they had begun to inquire for servants, that the distinctive characteristics of the abode they had chosen was borne in upon them. Upon making inquiry, they gathered that the house had been occupied by three successive sets of tenants, all of whom complained that it was haunted by a dark, evil, whispering face, which lurked in dusky corners, met them in lonely rooms, or hung over the beds, terrifying the awakened sleepers.

This silent, flitting presence foretold death, for each family had left hurriedly and in deep distress upon the loss of one of its members; but as the drains and the roof were sound, and it has been definitely decided that the English law can take no account of ghosts, the Hendriks found themselves obliged to stick to their bargain. Finally, the Colonel, who was a widower, secured the services of a gaunt Scotch housekeeper, professing herself well acquainted with the habits of ghosts, and thereupon took up his residence with his son at № 1, being fully persuaded that a free use of shooting-irons was likely to prove as good a preventive against hauntings as against any other form of annoyance.

Three days later, on the 5th February, the first symptoms of disturbance set in. The Hendriks had been out very late, and on their return, in the small hours, found their housekeeper scared and shaking, and with a circumstantial story to tell of the apparition. She said she had been awakened from sleep by the touch of a death-cold hand. Opening her eyes, she saw a fearsome, whispering face hanging over her; she could not catch the meaning of the words it said, but was persuaded that they were of a threatening nature.

A faint light flickered about the face, "like I've seen brandy on a dish of raisins," continued Miss Anderson, "and I could see it was wrapped up in its winding-sheet, gone yellow wi' age and lying by. At last the light went out like a flash, and I lay trembling in the dairk till I heard the latch-key in the door, for I was fair frechtened at yon ghaist." One further detail she added, to the effect that on going to bed she had locked the door and put the key under her pillow, where she found it safe after the visit of the apparition, although the door was still fast locked when she tried to leave the room an hour later.

After this experience the Americans had all the bolts and locks of the house examined and strengthened, also one or other of them remained at home every evening.

It was in the course of the following week that young Lamartine Hendriks went out to a theatre, leaving his father at home. He was absent something over three hours and a half. When he returned between eleven and twelve o'clock, he found Colonel Hendriks sitting at the table in the dining-room, his body swollen to an enormous size, his face of a livid indigo, and quite dead. Calling down the housekeeper, the young man went for a doctor. He recollected having seen a doctor's plate on the door of a house in a shabby street close by. Dr. Mulroon was at home—a big, powerful Irishman, rather the worse for liquor, but with the deep eye and square jaw that indicate ability. Hendriks hurried him round to Karma Crescent. On the way Mulroon asked no questions; he walked silently into the dining-room and looked steadily at the Colonel. Then he shook his head.

"Bedad! It's just what I expected!" he said.

"What?" asked Hendriks sharply.

Mulroon was sober enough by this time.

"It's the old story," he replied, with a strong brogue. "This makes the fourth case of the same kind I've been called in to see in this house during the last eighteen months."

"In this neighbourhood, you mean?"

"In this house, faith, and nowhere else! Didn't ye know it was haunted? Haven't you heard of the 'Strange Deaths in South London?' The papers had them in capitals an inch long."

Hendriks leant against the table and spoke hoarsely.

"We have just come from America, and I can recall something of what you mention, but I did not connect them with this house. As you have attended similar cases, tell me what is the cause of death?"

"The Public Analyst himself couldn't do that, by Jove! Not in the way you want to hear it. I made an examination in each case as well as he, and maybe I'm as capable as he of finding out the cause—perhaps more so! For I swept off every medal and honour that came in my way at Dublin, and—but what's the use of talking? No man living can tell you more than this. The blue colour of the tissues and the swelling are produced by a change in the condition of the blood, though the most exhaustive examination has failed to discover any reason for such a change. The result is death, that is the only certainty about it!"

A long silence ensued, and then Hendriks said quietly: "If it takes me to the last day of my life, I'll get at this business from the inside. I'll never give it up until I know everything!"

"Well, now, look here, Mr. Hendriks, will you take my advice? The police and the doctors have done their living best over this business, and they're just where they were at the beginning. There's only one man in Europe can help you—Flaxman Low, the psychologist."

But Hendriks demurred, on the ground of having seen enough of such gentry in the States.

"Low is not like any of them, you may take my word for it. He is as sensible and as practical a man as you or I. I know what he can do, and how he sets about doing it, for I was in practice in the country four or five years ago, and he came down there and cleared up a mystery that had bothered the neighbourhood for above ten years. Leave this room exactly as it is. Wire for him first—you can get the police in after."

The upshot of this conversation was that Mr. Low arrived at Karma Crescent soon after it became light, having been fetched by Mulroon in person.

The dining-room was a square room, opening on to the garden by a French window. It was richly furnished, everything was in order, there was no sign of a struggle. At the table about ten feet from the glass doors sat the dead man—a disfigured and horrible spectacle. The body was inclined to the left, the head dropped rather forward on the left shoulder, the left arm hanging straight down at his side, and the left trouser leg slightly turned up. Low bent over him and looked at the puffed blue lips.

"Does the attitude suggest anything to you?" asked Flaxman Low after some time.

"He was bending forward to get his breath," returned Mulroon.

"On the contrary, he had been stooping forward and to the left, but leant back for relief when the final spasm seized him," said Low. "Whatever may have been the cause of death, its action was rapid. Now, can you give me the details of the former deaths which have taken place here?"

"I can do that same." Mulroon drew out a pocket-book. "Here you are.

"The first tenant of this house was Dr. Philipson Vines (D.D., you understand). On the 16th November 1889 he was found dead sitting in that same chair by the servants at 6:30 A.M. A fine edition of Froissart was open on the table before him. He had evidently been dead for several hours. His age was fifty-three, the body was well nourished, and all the organs healthy.

"Next, Richard Stephen Holding, a retired linendraper, with a large family, took the house. On the 3rd February 1890 he was found dead by his wife at 2 A.M. He also was seated at the table, and in the same attitude you have noticed in Colonel Hendrik's case. Like the Colonel, he was still warm. His age was sixty-three, and a progressive heart trouble existed—which was not, however, the cause of death.

"Next, the house was taken by a widow lady named Findlater, with one daughter and an invalid son. The son kept to his bedroom during the first fortnight of their stay, but one warm May morning he ventured down here. His sister left him in an armchair at 11:45 in the forenoon, and on returning half an hour after to bring him some beef-tea, she found him seated at the table, blue and swollen and dead, just like the others. Findlater was twenty-seven, and must in any case have died shortly from phthisis."

"Can you recollect the attitudes of the bodies when you saw them?"

"Only in the case of Holding. The two others had been laid on the couch before my arrival," answered Mulroon.

"Have you observed this left trouser leg?" continued Low.

"Yes, pulled up; it was the same with Holding's. Probably a convulsive clutch at the last moment, and, no doubt, involuntary."

Some further conversation having taken place, it was eventually arranged that Mr. Low should return in the evening to spend a few days with young Hendriks, and to study the surroundings.

After he had gone notice of the death was given and the usual formalities were carried out. The police examined the whole house, but so far as could be judged by prolonged searching, no one from outside could have got in, yet Colonel Hendriks had been done to death, although no wound appeared upon the body.

The evidence of Miss Anderson at the inquest excited much attention. Several persons interested in psychical mysteries were present and made copious notes, besides cross-examining the housekeeper subsequently at great length. But no one, police, doctors, or psychists, had any workable theory to offer. Miss Anderson stated before the coroner that she wished to leave № 1 Karma Crescent at once, as she was firmly persuaded that the malignant whispering face, which hung over her while she lay in bed, was the face of the "Wicked One."

The jury returned an open verdict, and Hendriks walked back to his house feeling very dejected. His father's unaccountable death weighed upon him. He could not rid himself of the remembrance of the hideously changed aspect of the keen, handsome face that had been so much to him from his boyhood.

He knew that Flaxman Low had been present unofficially at the inquest, and resolved to question him on arrival. But when Low came, he declined to commit himself to any opinion, though he went so far as to say that he hoped some further information might soon be forthcoming. And with this Hendriks had to be satisfied.

"I should like to occupy your late housekeeper's room, where, I understand, several manifestations have taken place," continued Mr. Low, "and if you would allow it to be understood that I am merely a servant, whom you have hired for the time being to attend upon you, I think it might be a wise precaution."

During the next few days Flaxman Low was busy. He had brought with him a number of solid and peculiar bolts, which he fixed on the various doors and windows, it seemed, almost at random. He shut off the basement very securely, and put another bolt on the *outside* of the shutters enclosing the glass doors leading from the dining-room into the garden. Yet, after all, Hendriks noticed that he went to bed for several nights leaving one or other of these fittings unbolted.

Meanwhile, Low loitered about the garden, and inside and outside the house. He walked over to the railway junction, and lingered in the little lane. He visited the unpleasant colony of houses by the river, and altogether gained a pretty thorough knowledge of the neighbourhood.

“Has that garden door from the lane been much used since you came here?” he asked Hendriks one morning.

“No; my father thought that, under the circumstances, it had better be secured. It was never used. And, as there is no cellarage, I don’t see how any persons can enter the house except after the ordinary style of the burglar, of which we have so far discovered no trace.”

Mulroon dropped in very often to see them, and one night he inquired of Flaxman Low if the apparition had made its appearance.

To the astonishment of both his companions, Mr. Low replied in the affirmative.

“What did you do?” asked Mulroon.

“Nothing,” replied Mr. Low. “My plans do not admit of any overt action yet. But I can assure you that Miss Anderson is a good observer; she gave us a very correct description of its appearance.”

“Then it was an evil spirit?”

Mr. Flaxman Low smiled a little. “Undoubtedly,” he said.

That night Mr. Low securely bolted off the basement from the upper floor. He had since his coming insisted that no one but himself should enter the dining-room at any time or for any purpose. He begged that it should be neither ventilated nor aired, but left closed and unopened. Every day he went in and remained for some time, morning and evening. On this occasion he paid the room his usual nightly visit, and Hendriks from the hall could hear him locking the French windows.

“Won’t you draw your patent safety bolt outside, too?” he called out. “You’ve forgotten that every night.”

"I think I may leave that for the present," was Low's reply.

"There's nothing to be got out of you, Mr. Low," said Hendriks with some irritation.

"Not yet, but I hope soon to have something to say for myself," Flaxman Low answered.

On the next day Mr. Low did not visit the dining-room until the afternoon. He opened the doors to air the room, and lit the fire, after which he unlocked the French windows, and, shutting the door behind him, went to speak to Hendriks in the next room.

"I am going out for a short time," he said. "Will you be good enough not to enter the dining-room during my absence? Mulroon will probably come round. Please warn him also."

It was already growing dark when Mr. Low left the house. He remained away but a short time, and on his return was much disturbed by hearing Mulroon's big voice arguing with Hendriks in the dining-room. He opened the door. Mulroon was sitting in the same high-backed chair in which Colonel Hendriks had met his death. The Irishman was a little tipsy, and, in consequence, annoyingly obstinate.

Mr. Low laid down the basket he held in his hand.

"For heaven's sake, Mulroon, don't move! If you do, you're a dead man!" he said, approaching him. "Now, keep your legs straight—so, and rise gently."

Mulroon, grumbling a good deal, but partially sobered by Flaxman Low's manifest alarm, did as he was told.

"Now," added Low, "if you will kindly leave me for a few minutes alone, I will join you later."

Mulroon, however, had patients to attend to, and left the house, so that when Mr. Low followed Hendriks into the drawing-room a quarter of an hour afterwards, he found the American alone.

"There were two questions which I set myself to answer when I came to this house," said Low. "One was—Why did these persons die? There was a peculiar and obscure cause, of which we saw the effects. The second was—By whose agency were these persons subjected to the cause of death? I have partially solved one problem to-night. To-morrow I have some hope of reaching the other. To begin with, I have already satisfied myself as to the precise manner of death. To-morrow night, if you and Mulroon will meet me here, I will tell you, as far as I can, how the whole mystery may be solved."

All the next day Flaxman Low and Hendriks kept close to the house. After dark Flaxman Low disappeared, and had not returned by eleven o'clock. Mulroon and Hendriks sat waiting for him in the drawing-room, until presently he walked into the room, and threw himself into an arm-chair.

"I think now," he said, "that I may venture to say that I have something to show you.

"To begin at the beginning, this house was declared by successive tenants to be haunted. Further, the manifestations were said to be connected in some way with the deaths that took place after the apparitions had been seen—in all cases by some member of the household other than the victim. Whether these saw or heard anything prior to death was naturally beyond the power of their relatives to discover. But I fancy I can now answer that question. I have fairly good proof that they did not see any apparition."

"There never was any sign of a struggle or disturbance," put in Mulroon. "And that reminds me of what an old Irish charwoman, who worked here in the Findlaters' time, told me—that many cases had been known in her part of Ireland where the sight of a ghost turned the blood in the veins of the beholder. To be sure, we only smile at such sayings, but if you can give me any better reason why these men died, I'll thank you."

"This is exactly the point I hope to make," replied Low. "But to return to the manifestations. Miss Anderson's account of the ghost tallies with the stories of other residents. It nearly always appeared to the servants, by the way. The thing was evil, and whispered, and each was convinced they could have understood what it said had they not been too frightened to do so. Then all agreed in saying it wore its winding-sheet. This added strength to my first conclusion, and the further I pushed my inquiries the more I was confirmed in my theory."

"But the deaths. You cannot account for them?" asked Hendriks. "You can't persuade me that any whispering face killed my father. He would have put a bullet through it on sight."

"Pray be patient," said Flaxman Low. "You had very little data to go upon. In all cases the post-mortem aspect was the same—the terribly distended bodies, the puffy lips, the bluish skin. Something had brought about this aspect with its concurrent effect—death, but no one could find out anything more. Knowledge stopped at the ultimate fact of death. It appeared to be impossible to get behind that last wall."

Hendriks made a movement of impatience.

"Yes, yes, but where do the ghosts come in?"

"Nowhere," replied Flaxman Low decisively. "At a very early stage of the business I entirely cast aside all thoughts of spiritual phenomena. Two points, which I noticed in connection with Colonel Hendriks's appearance, aided me—the turning up of the left trouser leg, and the position of the body in the chair. From these two facts the conclusion was obvious. I then knew why the people had died. There was, of course, no ghost at all. They had simply been murdered!"

"By whom?" said Hendriks suddenly.

"But allow me to ask you what you deduced from the winding-sheet and the whisperings?" asked Mulroon.

"Taken in conjunction with the manner of death of the inmates of this house," said Flaxman Low, "I deduced a Chinaman. The winding-sheet meant simply loose garments, which might readily be nothing more than the formless wide-sleeved jacket of dirty yellow commonly worn by the Chinese. Upon this I searched the whole neighbourhood for a yellow skin, and came upon a furtive little colony down by the riverside."

"But we had this house secured in all sorts of ways. How could this fellow have gained an entrance, and what grudge can he bear against us? Then, as you know, there was no struggle."

"The reason of the haunting and the murders is evident. Certain persons want to keep this house empty for purposes of their own. They have some means of entering from the basement, and they are in possession of duplicate keys for every lock, a matter which reduces the haunting to a very simple process. If you remember, one of my very first steps was to fix bolts—which cannot be unlocked—upon some of the doors. I bolted off the basement for two nights after my arrival, and consequently I slept in peace. On the third night I left the dividing door locked only, and I was at once favoured with a glimpse of the whispering face lit up by the usual phosphorescent trick. As I expected, the face was of the Malay cast, and it threatened in mumbling pidgin English.

"You told me, Mr. Hendriks, that the garden door had not been opened since your tenancy began—that it was in fact secured. I had reason to think otherwise, and made certain of the correctness of my opinion by tying a thread across the doorway on the inner side, which was broken more than once. From the garden door to the French window in the dining-room was a natural step in my theory."

"But that bolt you put upon the outside of the wooden shutters?" said Mulroon.

"It suited my plans to put it there; in fact, I hope it is holding well at this moment. Knowing that duplicate keys existed, I presumed that some one would enter the dining-room shortly, for a purpose which I will presently explain. I therefore put up my little thread-detective inside the French window, and it also gave satisfactory evidence. Some one had entered the room, and to make sure of their motive for doing so, I purchased a rat, which I brought back in a basket with me last evening; but Mulroon very nearly saved me the trouble of trying any experiment on my own part by sitting down in the chair which seems to be the fatal one here."

Mulroon turned pale, and laughed in a forced manner.

"Well, well," he said, "the drink makes fools of us all, but my luck stood to me. How did I escape, Mr. Low?"

"You had the luck of long legs, that is all. When you sat in the chair, the backs of your knees did not come against the frame of the seat; if they had, you would have been in your coffin by now."

"Then you have discovered how my father met his death?" exclaimed Hendriks.

"Yes. In examining the chair, I found the legs had been neatly cut, so as to tilt back the chair at a slight angle, and any person sitting in it would naturally sit far back in consequence, thus bringing the back of the knees against the wooden bar in front of the seat. To the left of this bar I found a tiny splinter of steel fixed in, and I tried its effect last night upon a rat, with the result that it died almost immediately, its body being dreadfully swollen in the course of a few minutes. The turned-up trouser on the left leg led me directly to this discovery. To take the case of Colonel Hendriks, he felt the prick on the inner side of the left knee, and was turning up his trouser when the poison took effect, and he died in the act."

"I remember now that at the post-mortem examination you pointed out a hardly visible mark on the Colonel's knee," said Mulroon; "but it seemed too faint and tiny to afford any clue. But as you are in a position to prove that the persons who have died here have died of poison, can you account for the fact that no trace of poison has been discovered in any of the bodies?"

"Other known poisons disappear from the system in a similar manner. In this instance, guided by my supposition that the perpetrators of the murders were Chinese, I naturally set about finding out as much as possible about the subject of Chinese poisons. I cannot tell you the name, much less the specific nature of the poison used here, but I am prepared to show proofs that similar results have been recorded with regard to the victims of a certain terrible secret society in China, which owes much of its power and prestige to the fact that it can strike its opponents with the dreaded 'Blue Death.'"

"But we are as far as ever from finding the murderer," objected Hendriks. "To find him and punish him is all that I care for. Nothing else has the slightest interest for me!"

"I calculated," began Low, when this outburst was over, "I calculated that as the murderer had not yet accomplished his purpose of driving us out of the house, he would return to his diabolical work sooner or later. Hence I was quite cheered when the ghost visited me. I identified my man two days ago, but I waited to get an opportunity of bringing his crimes home to him. Will you come with me into the dining-room?"

Hendriks and Mulroon followed Flaxman Low, who carried a candle. For a second he listened at the door of the dining-room, but dead silence reigned. "I bolted the shutters of the windows on the outside after I had seen my man enter to renew the supply of poison on the steel point," said Flaxman Low. "I hope we may find him still here. He will probably make a dash at us. Will you be careful?"

"All right," said Hendriks, showing his revolver.

Low opened the door. Nothing moved inside the room, but sitting at the table was a huddled figure. The hat had fallen off, the head with its coiled pigtail lay upon the outstretched arms. Another moment made it clear that the man was dead. They lit the candles on the mantelpiece, and proceeded to examine the dead body.

The yellow face was puffed beyond recognition; the whole man was strangely and quiescently horrible. On the table before him lay a small lacquered box containing a scrap of a dark ointment, and in the man's forefinger was found a splinter of steel. Finding himself trapped, he had made away with himself rather than face his captors.

At this stage of the proceedings, Flaxman Low retired from the affair.

The police managed to hush up the business—the death of a Chinaman more or less makes little stir at any time,—and they had further investigations of importance to make which they wished to keep quiet.

It was, indeed, ultimately proved that № 1 Karma Crescent formed a very convenient headquarters for Chinese and other ruffianism, being situated as it was near a junction, near the river, and near a low part of London. It was found that extensive excavations had been made in communication with the house, and a well-built tunnel opened by a cleverly masked entrance into the lane. Thus by Flaxman Low's efforts a very distinct danger had been warded off, for the society in question were making very alarming headway in London, chiefly by allying themselves with other bands of criminals in this country, to whom they offered a secure place of hiding.

THE STORY OF KONNOR OLD HOUSE

"I hold," Mr. Flaxman Low was saying, "that there are no other laws in what we term the realm of the supernatural but those which are the projections or extensions of natural laws."

"Very likely that's so," returned Naripse, with suspicious humility. "But, all the same, Konnor Old House presents problems that won't work in with any natural laws I'm acquainted with. I almost hesitate to give voice to them, they sound so impossible and—and absurd."

"Let's judge of them," said Low.

"It is said," said Naripse, standing up with his back to the fire, "it is said that a Shining Man haunts the place. Also a light is frequently seen in the library—I've watched it myself of a night from here; yet the dust there, which happens to lie very thick over the floor and the furniture, has afterwards shown no sign of disturbance."

"Have you satisfactory evidence of the presence of the Shining Man?"

"I think so," replied Naripse shortly. "I saw him myself the night before I wrote asking you to come up to see me. I went into the house after dusk, and was on the stairs when I saw him: the tall figure of a man, absolutely white and shining. His back was towards me, but the sullen, raised shoulders and sidelong head expressed a degree of sinister animosity that exceeded anything I've ever met with. So I left him in possession, for it's a fact that any one who has tried to leave his card at Konnor Old House has left his wits with it."

"It certainly sounds rather absurd," said Mr. Low, "but I suppose we have not heard all about it yet?"

"No, there is a tragedy connected with the house, but it's quite a commonplace sort of story, and in no way accounts for the Shining Man."

Naripse was a young man of means, who spent most of his time abroad, but the above conversation took place at the spot to which he always referred as home—a shooting-lodge connected with his big grouse-moor on the west coast of Scotland. The lodge was a small new house built in a damp valley, with a trout-stream running just beyond the garden-hedge.

From the high ground above, where the moor stretched out towards the Solway Firth, it was possible on a fine day to see the dark cone of Ailsa Craig rising above the shimmering ripples. But Mr. Low happened to arrive in a spell of bad weather, when nothing was visible about the lodge but a few roods of sodden lowland, and a curve of the yellow tumbling little river, and beyond a mirky outline of shouldering hills blurred by the ever-falling rain. It may have been eleven o'clock on a depressing, muggy night, when Naripse began to talk about Konnor Old House, as he sat with his guests over a crackling flaming fire of pinewood.

"Konnor Old House stands on a spur of the ridge opposite—one of the finest sites possible, and it belongs to me.

Yet I am obliged to live in this damp little bog-hole, for the man who would pass a night in Konnor is not to be met with in this county!"

Sullivan, the third man present, replied he was, perhaps—with a glance at Low—there were two, which stung Naripse, who turned his words into a deliberate challenge.

"Is it a bet?" asked Sullivan, rising. He was a tallish man, dark, and clean-shaven, whose features were well known to the public in connection with the emerald green jersey of the Rugby International Football Team of Ireland. "If it is, it's a bet I'm going to win! Good night. In the morning, Naripse, I'll trouble you for the difference."

"The affair is much more in Low's line than in yours," said Naripse. "But you're not really going?"

"You may take it I am, though!"

"Don't be a fool, Jack! Low, tell him not to go, tell him there are things no man ought to meddle with——" he broke off.

"There are things no man can meddle with," replied Sullivan, obstinately fixing his cap on his head, "and my backing out of this bet would stand in as one of them!"

Naripse was strangely urgent.

"Low, speak to him! You know——"

Flaxman Low saw that the big Irishman's one vanity had got upon its legs; he also saw that Naripse was very much in earnest.

"Sullivan's big enough to take care of himself," he said, laughing. "At the same time, if he doesn't object, we might as well hear the story before he starts."

Sullivan hesitated, then flung his cap into a corner.

"That's so," he said.

It was a warm night for the time of the year, and they could hear, through the open window, the splashing downpour of the rain.

"There's nothing so lonely as the drip of heavy rain!" began Naripse, "I always associate it with Konnor Old House. The place has stood empty for ten years or more, and this is the story they tell about it. It was last inhabited by a Sir James Mackian, who had been a merchant of sorts in Sierra Leone. When the baronetcy fell in to him, he came to England and settled down in this place with a pretty daughter and a lot of servants, including a nigger, named Jake, whose life he was said to have saved in Africa. Everything went on well for nearly two years, when Sir James had occasion to go to Edinburgh for a few days. During his absence his daughter was found dead in her bed, having taken an overdose of some sleeping-draught. The shock proved too great for her father. He tried travelling, but on his return home he fell into a settled melancholy, and died some months later, a dumb imbecile, at the asylum."

"Well, I shan't object to meeting the girl as she's so pretty," remarked Sullivan, with a laugh. "But there's not much in the story."

"Of course," added Naripse, "countryside gossip adds a good deal of colour to the plain facts of the case. It is said that terrible details connected with Miss Mackian's death were suppressed at the inquest, and people recollected afterwards that for months the girl had worn an unhappy, frightened look. It seemed she disliked the negro, and had been heard to beg her father to send him away, but the old man would not listen to any suggestion of the kind."

"What became of the negro in the end," asked Flaxman Low.

"In the end Sir James kicked him out after a violent scene, in the course of which he appears to have accused Jake of having caused the girl's death. The nigger swore he'd be revenged on him, but, as a matter of fact, he left the place almost immediately, and has never been heard of since—which disposes of the nigger. A short time after the old man went mad: he was found lying on a couch in the library—a hopeless imbecile." Saying this, Naripse went to the window, and looked out into the rainy darkness. "Konnor Old House stands on the ridge opposite, and a part of the building, including the library window, where the light is sometimes seen, is visible through the trees from here. There is no light there to-night, though."

Sullivan laughed his big, full laugh.

"How about your Shining Man? I hope we may have the luck to meet. I suspect some canny Scots tramp knows where to get a snug roost rent free."

"That may be so," replied Naripse, with a slow patience. "I can only say that after seeing the light of a night, I have more than once gone up in the morning to have a look at the library, and never found the thick dust in the least disturbed."

"Have you noticed if the light appears at regular intervals?" said Low.

"No; it's there on and off. I generally see it in rainy weather."

"What sort of people have gone crazy in Konnor Old House?" asked Sullivan.

"One was a tramp. He must have lived pleasantly in the kitchens for days. Then he took to the library, which didn't agree with him, apparently. He was found in a dying state lying upon Sir James's couch, with horrible black patches on his face. He was too far gone to speak, so nothing was gleaned from him."

"He probably had a dirty face to start with, and having caught cold in the rain, went into Konnor Old House and died quietly there of pneumonia or something of the kind, just as you or I might have done, tucked up in our own little beds at home," commented Sullivan.

"The last man to try his luck with the ghosts," went on Naripse, without noticing this remark, "was a young fellow called Bowie, a nephew of Sir James. He was a student at Edinburgh University, and he wanted to clear up the mystery. I was not at home, but my factor allowed him to pass a night in the house. As he did not appear next day, they went to look for him. He was found lying on the couch—and he has not spoken a rational word since."

"Sheer, mere physical fright, acting on an overwrought brain!" Sullivan summed up the case scornfully. "And now I'm off. The rain has stopped, and I'll get up to the house before midnight. You may expect me at dawn to tell you what I've seen."

"What do you intend to do when you get there?" asked Flaxman Low.

"I'll pass the night on the ghostly couch, which I suppose I shall find in the library. Take my word for it, madness is in Sir James's family; father and daughter and nephew all gave proof of it in different ways. The tramp, who was perhaps in there for a couple of days, died a natural death. It only needs a healthy man to run the gauntlet and set all this foolish talk at rest."

Naripse was plainly much disturbed, though he made no further objection; but when Sullivan was gone, he moved restlessly about the room, looking out of the window from time to time. Suddenly he spoke—

"There it is! The light I mentioned to you."

Mr. Low went to the window. Away on the opposite ridge a faint light glimmered out through the thick gloom. Then he glanced at his watch.

"Rather over an hour since he started," he remarked. "Well now, Naripse, if you will be so good as to hand me *Human Origins* from the shelf behind you, I think we may settle down to wait for dawn. Sullivan's just the man to give a good account of himself—under most circumstances."

"Heaven send there may be no black side to this business!" said Naripse. "Of course, I was a fool to say what I did about the Old House, but nobody except an ass like Jack would think I meant it. I wish the night was well over! That light is due to go out in two hours anyway."

Even to Mr. Low the night seemed unbearably long; but at the first streak of dawn he tossed his book on to the sofa, stretched himself, and said: "We may as well be moving; let's go and see what Sullivan is doing."

The rain had begun to fall again, and was coming down in close straight lines as the two men drove up the avenue to Konnor Old House. As they ascended, the trees grew thicker on the banks of the cutting which led them in curves to the terrace on which stood the house. Although it was a modern red-brick building, rather picturesque with gables and sharply pitched overhanging roofs, it looked desolate and forbidding enough in the grey daybreak. To the left lay lawns and gardens, to the right the cliff fell away steeply to where the burn roared in spate some three hundred feet below. They drove round to the empty stables, and then hurried back to the house on foot by a path that debouched directly in front of the library window. Naripse stopped under it and shouted: "Hullo! Jack, where are you?"

But no answer came, and they went on to the hall door. The gloom of the wet dawning and the heavy smell of stagnant air filled the big hall as they looked round at its dreary emptiness. The silence within the house itself was oppressive. Again Naripse shouted, and the noise echoed harshly through the passages, jarring on the stillness. Then he led the way to the library at a run.

As they came in sight of the doorway, a wave of some nauseating odour met them, and at the same moment they saw Sullivan lying just outside the threshold, his body twisted and rigid like a man in the extremity of pain, his contorted profile ivory-pale against the dark oak flooring. As they stooped to raise him, Mr. Low had just time to notice the big gloomy room beyond, with its heaped and trampled layers of accumulated dust. There was no time for more than a glance, for the indescribable, fetid odour almost overpowered them as they hastened to carry Sullivan into the open air.

"We must get him home as soon as we can," said Mr. Low, "for we have a very sick man on our hands."

This proved to be true. But in a few days, thanks to Mr. Low's treatment and untiring care, the severe physical symptoms became less urgent, and in due time Sullivan's mind cleared.

The following account is taken from the written statement of his experience in Konnor Old House—

"On reaching the house he entered as noiselessly as possible, and made for the library, finding his way by the help of a series of matches to Sir James's couch, upon which he lay down. He was conscious at once of an acrid taste in his mouth, which he accounted for by the clouds of dust he had raised in crossing the room.

"First he began to think about the approaching football match with Scotland for which he was already in training. He was still in his mood of derisive incredulity. The house seemed vastly empty, and wrapped in an uneasy silence, a silence which made each of his comfortable movements an omen of significance. Presently the sense of a presence in the room was borne in upon him. He sat up and spoke softly. He almost expected some one to answer him, and so strong did this feeling become that he called out: 'Who's there?' No reply came, and he sat on amidst the oppressive silence. He says the slightest noise would have been a relief. It was the listening in the silence that bred in him so intense a longing to grapple with some solid opponent.

"Fear! He, who had denied the very existence of cause for fear, found himself shivering with an untranslatable terror! This was fear! He realised it with an infinite recoil of anger.

"Presently he became aware that the darkness about him was clearing. A feeble light filtered slowly through it from above. Looking up at the ceiling, he perceived directly above his head an irregular patch of pale phosphorescent luminance, which grew gradually brighter. How long he sat with his head thrown back, staring at the light, he does not know. It seemed years. Then he spoke to himself plainly. With an immense effort he forced his eyes away from the light and got upon his feet to drag his limbs round the room. The phosphorescence was of a greenish tint, and as strong as moonlight, but the dust rose like vapour at the slightest movement and somewhat obscured its power. He moved about, but not for long. A clogging weight, such as one feels in nightmare, pressed upon him, and his exhaustion was intensified by the overpowering physical disgust bred in him by the repulsive odour which passed across his face as he staggered back to the couch.

"For a few moments he would not look up. He says he had an impression that some one was watching him through the radiance as through a window. The atmosphere about him was thickening and cloaking the walls with drowsy horror, while his senses revolted and choked at the growing odour. Then followed a state of semi-sleep, for he recollects no more until he found himself staring again at the luminous patch on the ceiling.

"By this time the brightness was beginning to dim; dark smears showed through it here and there, which ran slowly together till out of them grew and protruded a fat, black, evil face. A second later Sullivan was aware that the horrible face was sinking down nearer and nearer to his own, while all about it the light changed to black, dripping fluid, that formed great drops and fell.

"It seemed as if he could not save himself; he could not move! The fighting blood in him had died out. Then fear, mad fear and strong loathing, gave him the strength to act. He saw his own hand working savagely; it passed through and through the impending face, yet he swears that he felt a slight impact and that he saw the fat, glazed skin quiver! Then, with a final struggle, he tore himself from the couch, and rushing to the door he wrenched it open, and plunged forward into a red vacancy, down—down—— After that he remembers no more."

While Sullivan still lay ill and unable to give an account of himself or of what had happened at Konnor Old House, Mr. Flaxman Low expressed his intention of paying a visit to the asylum for the purpose of seeing young Bowie. But on arrival at the asylum, he found that Bowie had died during the previous night. A weary-eyed assistant doctor took Mr. Low to see the body. Bowie had evidently been of a gaunt, but powerful build. The features, though harsh, were noble, the face being somewhat disfigured by a rough, raised discoloration, which extended from the centre of the forehead to behind the right ear.

Mr. Low asked a question.

"Yes, a very obscure case," observed the young doctor, "but it is the disease he died of. When he was brought here some months ago he had a small dark spot on his forehead, but it spread rapidly, and there are now similar large patches over the whole of his body. I take it to be of a cancerous character, likely to occur in a scrofulous subject after a shock and severe mental strain, such as Bowie chose to subject himself to by passing a night in Konnor Old House. The first result of the shock was imbecility, an increasingly lethargic condition of the body supervened, and finally coma."

While the doctor was speaking, Mr. Low bent over the dead man and closely examined the mark upon the face.

"This mark appears to be the result of a fungoid growth, perhaps akin to the Indian disease known as *mycetoma*," he said at length.

"It may be so. The case is very obscure, but the disease, whatever we may call it, appears to be in Bowie's family, for I believe his uncle, Sir James Mackian, had precisely similar symptoms during his last illness. He also died in this institution, but that was before my time," replied the assistant.

After a further examination of the body Mr. Low took his leave, and during the following day or two was busily engaged in a spare empty room placed at his disposal by Naripse. A deal table and chair were all he required, Mr. Low explained, and to these he added a microscope, an apparatus for producing a moist heat, and the coat worn by Sullivan on the night of his adventure. At the end of the third day, as Sullivan was already on the road to recovery, Mr. Low, accompanied by Naripse, paid a second visit to Konnor Old House, during which Low mentioned some of his conclusions about the strange events which had occurred there. It will be an easy task to compare Mr. Flaxman Low's theory with the experience detailed by Sullivan, and with the one or two subsequent discoveries that added something like confirmation to his conclusions.

Mr. Low and his host drove up as on the previous occasion, and stabled the horse as before. The day was dry, but grey, and the time the early afternoon. As they ascended the path leading to the house, Mr. Low remarked, after gazing up for a few seconds at the library window—

"That room has the air of being occupied."

"Why?—What makes you think so?" asked Naripse nervously.

"It is hard to say, but it produces that impression."

Naripse shook his head despondently.

"I've always noticed it myself," he returned. "I wish Sullivan were all right again and able to tell us what he saw in there. Whatever it was, it has nearly cost him his life. I don't suppose we shall ever know anything more definite about the matter."

"I fancy I can tell you," replied Low, "but let us get on into the library, and see what it looks like before we enter into the subject any further. By the way, I should advise you to tie your handkerchief over your mouth and nose before we go into the room."

Naripse, upon whom the events of the last few days had had a very strong effect, was in a state of scarcely-controllable excitement.

"What do you mean, Low?—you can't have any idea——"

"Yes, I believe the dust in the house to be simply poisonous. Sullivan inhaled any amount of it—hence his condition."

The same suggestion of loneliness and stagnation hung about the house as they passed through the hall and entered the library. They halted at the door and looked in. The amount of greenish dust in the room was extraordinary; it lay in little drifts and mounds over the floor, but most abundantly just about the couch. Immediately above this spot, they perceived on the ceiling a long, discoloured stain. Naripse pointed to it.

"Do you see that? It is a blood-stain, and, I give you my word, it grows larger and larger every year!" He finished the sentence in a low voice, and shuddered.

"Ah, so I should have expected," observed Flaxman Low, who was looking at the stained ceiling with much interest. "That, of course, explains everything."

"Low, tell me what you mean? A blood-stain that grows year by year explains everything?" Naripse broke off and pointed to the couch. "Look there! a cat's been walking over the sofa."

Mr. Low put his hand on his friend's shoulder and smiled.

"My dear fellow! that stain on the ceiling is simply a patch of mould and fungi. Now come in carefully without raising the dust, and let us examine the cat's footsteps, as you call them."

Naripse advanced to the couch and considered the marks gravely.

"They are not the footmarks of any animal, they are something much more unaccountable. They are raindrops. And why should raindrops be here in this perfectly water-tight room, and even then only in one small part of it? You can't very well explain that, and you certainly can't have expected it?"

"Look round and follow my points," replied Mr. Low. "When we came to fetch Sullivan, I noticed the dust, which far exceeds the ordinary accumulation even in the most neglected places. You may also notice that it is of a greenish colour and of extreme fineness. This dust is of the same nature as the powder you find in a puff-ball, and is composed of minute sporuloid bodies. I found that Sullivan's coat was covered with this fine dust, and also about the collar and upper portion of the sleeve I found one or two gummy drops which correspond to these raindrops, as you call them. I naturally concluded from their position that they had fallen from above. From the dust, or rather spores, which I found on Sullivan's coat, I have since cultivated no fewer than four specimens of fungi, of which three belong to known African species; but the fourth, so far as I know, has never been described, but it approximates most closely to one of the *phalliodei*."

"But how about the raindrops, or whatever they are? I believe they drop from that horrible stain."

"They are drops from the stain, and are caused by the unnamed fungus I have just alluded to. It matures very rapidly, and absolutely decays as it matures, liquefying into a sort of dark mucilage, full of spores, which drips down, and diffuses a most repulsive odour. In time the mucilage dries, leaving the dust of the spores."

"I don't know much about these things myself," replied Naripse dubiously, "and it strikes me you know more than enough. But, look here, how about the light? You saw it last night yourself."

"It happens that the three species of African fungi possess well known phosphorescent properties, which are manifested not only during decomposition, but also during the period of growth. The light is only visible from time to time; probably climatic and atmospheric conditions only admit of occasional efflorescence."

"But," objected Naripse, "supposing it to be a case of poisoning by fungi as you say, how is it that Sullivan, though exposed to precisely the same sources of danger as the others who have passed a night here, has escaped? He has been very ill, but his mind has already regained its balance, whereas, in the three other cases, the mind was wholly destroyed."

Mr. Low looked very grave.

"My dear fellow, you are such an excitable and superstitious person that I hesitate to put your nerves to any further test."

"Oh, go on!"

"I hesitate for two reasons. The one I have mentioned, and also because in my answer I must speak of curious and unpleasant things, some of which are proved facts, others only more or less well-founded assumptions. It is acknowledged that fungi exert an important influence in certain diseases, a few being directly attributable to fungi as a primary cause. Also it is an historical fact that poisonous fungi have more than once been used to alter the fate of nations. From the evidence before us and the condition of Bowie's body, I can but conclude that the unknown fungus I have alluded to is of a singularly malignant nature, and acts through the skin upon the brain with terrible rapidity, afterwards gradually interpenetrating all the tissues of the body, and eventually causing death. In Sullivan's case, luckily, the falling drops only touched his clothing, not his skin."

"But wait a minute, Low, how did these fungi come here? And how can we rid the house of them? Upon my word, it is enough to make a man go off his head to hear about it. What are you going to do now?"

"In the first place we will go upstairs and examine the flooring just above that stained patch of ceiling."

"You can't do that, I'm afraid. The room above this happens to be divided into two portions by a hollow partition between two feet and three feet thick," said Naripse, "the interior of which may originally have been meant for a cupboard, but I don't think it has ever been used."

"Then let us examine the cupboard; there must be some way of getting into it."

Upon this Naripse led the way upstairs, but as he gained the top he leant back, and, grasping Mr. Low by the arm, thrust him violently forward.

"Look! the light—did you see the light?" he said.

For a second or two it seemed as if a light, like the elusive light thrown by a rotating reflector, quivered on the four walls of the landing, then disappeared almost before one could be certain of having seen it.

"Can you point me out the precise spot where you saw the shining figure you told us of?" asked Low.

Naripse pointed to a dark corner of the landing.

"Just there, in front of that panel between the two doors. Now that I come to think of it, I fancy there is some means of opening the upper part of that panel. The idea was to ventilate the cupboard-like space I mentioned just now."

Naripse walked across the landing and felt round the panel, till he found a small metal knob. On turning this, the upper part of the panel fell back like a shutter, disclosing a narrow space of darkness beyond. Naripse thrust his head into the opening and peered into the gloom, but immediately started back with a gasp.

"The Shining Man!" he cried. "He's there!"

Mr. Flaxman Low, hardly knowing what to expect, looked over his shoulder; then, exerting his strength, pulled away some of the lower boarding. For within, at arm's length, stood a dimly shining figure!—a tall man, with his back towards them, leaning against the left side of the partition, and shrouded from head to foot in faintly luminous white mould.

The figure remained quite motionless while they stared at it in surprise; then Mr. Flaxman Low pulled on his glove, and, leaning forward, touched the man's head. A portion of the white mass came away in his fingers, the lower surface of which showed a bunch of frizzled negroid hair.

"Good heavens, Low, what do you make of this?" asked Naripse. "It must be the body of Jake. But what is this shining stuff?"

Low stood under the wide skylight and examined what he held in his fingers.

"Fungus," he said at last. "And it appears to have some property allied to the mouldy fungus which attacks the common house-fly. Have you not seen them dead upon window-panes, stiffly fixed upon their legs, and covered with a white mould? Something of the same kind has taken place here."

"But what had Jake to do with the fungus? And how did he come here?"

"All that, of course, we can only surmise," replied Mr. Low. "There is little doubt that secrets of nature hidden from us are well known to the various African tribes. It is possible that the negro possessed some of these deadly spores, but how or why he made use of them are questions that can never be cleared up now."

"But what was he doing here?" asked Naripse.

"As I said before, we can only guess the answer to that question, but I should suppose that the negro made use of this cupboard as a place where he could be free from interruption; that he here cultivated the spores is proved by the condition of his body and of the ceiling immediately below. Such an occupation is by no means free from danger, especially in an airless and enclosed space like this. It is evident that either by design or accident he became infected by the fungus poison, which in time covered his whole body as you now see. The subject of Obeah," Flaxman Low went on reflectively, "is one to the study of which I intend to devote myself at some future period. I have, indeed, already made some arrangements for an expedition in connection with the subject into the interior of Africa."

"And how is the horrible thing to be got rid of? Nothing short of burning the place down would be of any radical use," remarked Naripse.

Low, who by this time was deeply engrossed in considering the strange facts with which he had just become acquainted, answered abstractedly: "I suppose not."

Naripse said no more, and the words were only recalled to Mr. Low's mind a day or two later, when he received by post a copy of the *West Coast Advertiser*. It was addressed in the handwriting of Naripse, and the following extract was lightly scored:—

> "Konnor Old House, the property of Thomas Naripse, Esquire, of Konnor Lodge, was, we regret to say, destroyed by fire last night. We are sorry to add that the loss to the owner will be considerable, as no insurance policy had been effected with regard to the property."

THE STORY OF CROWSEDGE

A fixed aversion to notoriety is one of Mr. Flaxman Low's most marked characteristics. Had this not been so, he would undoubtedly have formed the subject of many an interview in the illustrated magazines. But his manner of life and pursuits set him apart from the common lot, and he stands aloof, a solitary and interesting figure surrounded by his books, his Egyptian treasures, and his grotesque memories, a man who has dived deep into the past and also explored daringly beyond the borders of that vast realm of mystery, of which the public catch but a very slight glimpse through the medium of these stories.

Athlete, Egyptologist, and psychical student, his is a strangely blended existence, at one moment breathing the mental atmosphere of the Sixth Dynasty, the next hour perhaps fighting single-handed some fearless battle against an opponent from whom the bravest need find no shame in accepting defeat. But Flaxman Low is a man who finds defeat intolerable; with him there is no end to a struggle, he will pursue the interpretation of a tough linguistic problem in exactly the same spirit as he applies himself to the elucidation of the most baffling and dangerous psychical phenomena. Yet this unassuming English gentleman, who combines in his own personality the reckless courage of a Regency blood and the knowledge of a profound scholar, is best known among his friends for his kind smile and the genial help he is ready to offer in every case of need.

The following story differs from those which have gone before it in that it does not deal solely with the mystery of some haunted spot; it draws across the page another figure, possessing in a high degree the intellectual grasp, the wide knowledge, and the exhaustive will-power which distinguish Mr. Low, but using them for very different purposes.

In the beginning of 1893 Dr. Kalmarkane first rose upon the horizon of Mr. Low's life. Any detailed history of the transactions between them is here impossible, but a slight sketch of one or two of the principal incidents may not be altogether out of place. Up to January 1893 Mr. Low had very little knowledge of Dr. Kalmarkane beyond the fact that he was a man of extraordinary ability, whose researches had led him deeply into those very recesses of knowledge, to the exploration of which Mr. Low has given up his own life. He also knew that it was Kalmarkane's habit to visit town occasionally, to stalk about for a couple of days on the pavements, to drop in upon psychical meetings, where he would listen to the proceedings with a face of sour scorn, and then to plunge back into the obscurity of his lonely life in some remote corner of the Isle of Purbeck.

The more intimate dealings between these great rivals began on a winter night when a thin powdering of snow lay upon the London pavements. For three days banks of swollen yellowish-grey clouds had rolled up slowly before a north wind that cut round every corner. It was already late, and Mr. Flaxman Low was sitting alone in his chambers in Fassifern Court, when a gentleman was shown up, who carried in with him something of the rawness of the night outside.

The visitor, as he threw back his thick ulster, showed a young, slim, and well-formed figure; then he flicked a flake or two of snow from his small, black imperial, and stood in some embarrassment opposite to Mr. Low.

"Do you remember a fresher, who came up to Oxford the year you left, of the name of d'lmiran?" he said.

Mr. Flaxman Low extended his hand.

"You must forgive me," he said. "The hair on your face alters you a good deal. I recollect meeting you very often at your cousin's rooms, and, believe me, I am very heartily glad to see you. Where is Field? Still in China?"

Mr. Low now had time to look at his visitor. He saw that d'lmiran's eyes were restless, and that he seemed worn out for want of sleep.

"Yes, bug-hunting up the Hoang-ho when last I heard of him," replied d'Imiran perfunctorily. Then fixing his dark eyes on Mr. Low, he added: "Mr. Low, I have been driven here to-night by the sheer necessity of sharing a secret with some human soul. Do you happen to know Dr. Kalmarkane? He is a hirsute giant, with a tremendous frame, raw-boned, and ungainly. He has a long, strong, fleshy nose, a shock head of dark grey hair, and a ragged beard, which he is in the habit of twisting into spirals as he talks."

"I know something of him."

"You can't know him as I do. I have spent the last six months in his house. I dare say you fail to see why that fact should send me to disturb you at 10:30, but——"

Flaxman Low had in the meantime been attending to the wants of his guest. As d'Imiran paused, he smiled.

"My dear d'Imiran," he said, "I would gladly get up in the middle of my beauty-sleep to offer my sympathy to any man who had spent six months with Kalmarkane. Pray, tell me what I can do for you."

"I have been twenty-seven weeks under his roof," went on d'Imiran, "and I can only tell you that I have grown to dislike the man more every day of that time. There are mysteries about him; but you will hear enough of them if you will allow me to tell you my story. I know that I am straining your forbearance in coming to you with this tale; I know I have no right to ask you to listen to me, and I am almost afraid that at the end of it all I shall find you laughing at me. But I thought you were my best chance. There is no other man in London who would hear half a dozen sentences without advising me to see a nerve specialist and knock off work. But I assure you there is nothing whatever wrong with me in that way. I have not been overworking, though I admit that for the last six weeks the pressure of what I am about to tell you has bothered me."

"I am entirely at your service, and I promise to give you as fair a hearing as possible," said Low. "Am I right in supposing that you have studied medicine?"

D'Imiran nodded.

"I won the Scully Scholarship, which took me round the European schools of medicine. I have been house-surgeon at St. Martha's, and I have passed various necessary—and unnecessary—exams. About a year ago I felt that I must begin to turn some of the knowledge I had in my head into coin, and a friend of mine, knowing what I wanted, introduced me to Dr. Kalmarkane, who happened to be in need of an assistant with my qualifications to aid him for a time in his researches.

"The terms he offered me were good, so good that I accepted his proposal, and went down in June to Dorset, where he lives in a lonely house, called Crowsedge. It lies between miles of empty heath and miles of sand dunes. There Kalmarkane leads the life of a savage, a half-blind and almost idiotic old crone being the only creature he can get to serve him in the whole countryside, where he bears a most evil reputation; and the sight of his huge figure, swinging a heavy yellow cane, is enough to make people take to the bypaths to avoid him. If I were to repeat the many anecdotes which his self-centred and morose habits have given rise to, I should keep you up into the small hours. But I will hurry on as quickly as I can into the core of my story.

"Kalmarkane is, in fact, a sullen savage, who works eighteen hours out of the twenty-four, and the range of his knowledge is almost incredible. The object of his studies is a secret he keeps in his own brain, and I may say I have never fathomed its precise nature. Once or twice I put out a feeler to discover in what direction our researches were leading us, but I was met with a black look and a monosyllabic reply. At last on one occasion he told me that I was merely a hired servant, and that he did not pay me to pry into his affairs.

"This was in September, just before he started for Jutland, to be present at the opening of some tumuli belonging to the Bronze Age. However, he smoothed the thing over with a sort of apology, and begged me to remain. After his return Kalmarkane's attitude towards me altered. He allowed me to go further into every investigation, until, in fact, we trenched upon things with which I plainly refused to have anything to do. He towered over me with gripping hands as if he could have killed me, then he conquered himself and laughed: 'I believed you to be a man with a true love of knowledge, and I must remind you of Professor Clifford's words, "that it is wrong, always, everywhere, and for any one to believe anything upon insufficient evidence,"' he said. 'You and I are merely searching for the truth, Mr. d'Imiran, but I will for the future remember your susceptibilities. I myself think that your prejudice is an almost inconceivable survival of the mediæval superstition that certain kinds of knowledge are unlawful.' I replied that there were certain methods of acquiring knowledge which were certainly unlawful!"

D'Imiran paused and drew his handkerchief across his white lips.

"We were, and for that matter are, engaged in carrying out various investigations which bear upon an obscure subject. You, of course, know Kalmarkane's work on *Potencies of Etheric Energy*, dealing with the subject from the standpoint that such energies are excited and may be controlled by the mental condition. You can imagine where this might lead one——"

"I am acquainted with the book."

"Now pray consider what I am about to tell you as possible fact," continued d'Imiran, "though I confess that without the evidence of my own senses I could not have been brought to regard the thing in that light. After this conversation I became aware that Kalmarkane had grown to dislike me in a positive and malignant manner, which he nevertheless took pains to hide. Now I come to the point of my story. I have only two separate and not necessarily connected facts to put before you, both of which, however, go to prove that Kalmarkane is possessed of strange powers.

"Crowsedge is built on to a little square tower, which is probably of much older date than the house itself. The upper part of the tower serves Kalmarkane as a study, while the lower portion is a bare, damp, flagged space. The connecting stairs are of stone, very steep and narrow, which lead through a hole cut in the study floor on to a small partitioned landing. One side of these steps is attached to the wall, the other is unprotected by even a handrail, so that a slip or fall would send you headlong on to the flags below. One evening Kalmarkane, who was in my laboratory, sent me to fetch some papers from the tower. I had never before been allowed to enter the study alone.

"I carried a candle, and must mention that I was wearing a knickerbocker suit, with shoes, not boots. I found the papers at once, and at the same time happened to notice an ancient oblong box, which Kalmarkane had obtained from the tumuli in Jutland. It was lying on the floor, open and empty. When I was returning down the steps an unaccountable incident occurred. I have explained to you the position of that flight of steps. On my right there was the blank wall, on my left an open space, and I was about fourteen feet from the ground.

"I fancied I heard some one moving, and holding my candle over my head, I bent and looked down into the square, flagged room below. As I did so, a hand suddenly grasped my left ankle, and jerked me off my feet with a violent wrench. I crashed down on to the flags, and by what good escaped having my neck broken I luck I can't say. I put out my hands to save my head and pitched on my shoulder, and so got off with a severe shaking. Now, Mr. Low, I contend that no human arm could have reached me in the position I have described to you!"

"What had Kalmarkane to say about it?" asked Flaxman Low.

"He insisted that I had slipped in some way. I felt it better to seem to accept that explanation. But look here," and d'Imiran pulled down his sock, "I did not show him that!"

Upon the ankle was the distinct mark of a thumb and fingers clearly outlined in bruises.

"Will you notice one peculiarity about this?" said d'Imiran. "You perceive that it is the mark of a small hand, the grasp is short, the fingers slender, yet you can judge of its extraordinary strength."

"Now for the other incident," said Mr. Low.

"Next day I was at work as usual, but I could not sleep. I had a perpetual horror of that grasping hand. Then followed a most extraordinary coincidence, if it can never be proved to be anything more. I have told you that I had never entered Kalmarkane's study alone excepting on the one occasion immediately before my fall. A day or two later Kalmarkane had gone out for one of his long rambles over the heath, when I found myself at a standstill while making some notes, for I wished to verify a passage from an old treatise on alchemy, which Kalmarkane had carried off to his study during the morning. For a few minutes I hesitated. It was early in the afternoon, and recollecting that he had already sent me there, I decided on finding out if the study door were open, and if so, to take it as a sign that Kalmarkane would have no objection to my going in.

"I passed along the passage which led to the tower, and went up the steps, and as the handle turned quite easily, I went in. I saw the treatise I had come for at once. It lay on the further side of the table, just beyond the box I had noticed before. I bent across to get the book, and in doing so I perceived something in the box which startled me.

"Inside lay a human hand and part of a forearm. From its size I judged it to be the hand of a woman. It was brown and rough-skinned, and the wrist bore a bronze bracelet. I noticed that the bracelet was a ring open at one side, and decorated by those combinations of straight and curved lines so characteristic of the Bronze Age. Crowsedge, I must tell you, is full of the singular paraphernalia indispensable for studies such as Kalmarkane's, and odds and ends of humanity were not very unusual.

"But there was something in the appearance of this hand lying there, sienna-brown upon the discoloured cloths, that gave a horrible suggestion of life! It was resting back upwards with half-closed fingers, the muscles and flesh rising firmly over the bones. At the point of scission the surface was drawn and dried, so that separation from the body was not of recent date. I give you all these details in full, and I can swear to them. By chance, or, perhaps, out of curiosity, I touched the hand, and—it was warm!

"I declare to you that hand and arm felt in every particular like living flesh! I was still stooping over it, when I heard a sound behind me, and looked up to find Kalmarkane glaring at me with a diabolical expression. 'What are you doing here?' he roared. I answered that I was examining the hand. He shut down the lid of the box with a sharp movement. 'That severed hand has a history,' he said, with a sinister laugh. 'It has let out many a man's life, and—who knows?'

"That little incident decided me. I came up to town for a few days, and I felt impelled to-night, before returning to Crowsedge, to come and tell you all about it."

Mr. Low was silent for some time, then he asked—

"It is a very strange story, but I should be sorry to say it was not a true one. Put into plain words, you wish me to understand that Dr. Kalmarkane possesses a hand and arm, presumably, from the ornament upon it, belonging to some prehistoric man or woman of the Bronze Age; that this human remnant is endowed with life, and further, putting certain facts together, you are inclined to think that Kalmarkane can use this hand for his own purposes?"

D'Imiran heard Low out with his face buried in his hands. After Low had ceased speaking, however, he raised his head and replied—

"Put in that bald and blunt fashion, it sounds nothing more or less than the worst kind of madness!" he said despondently, "yet I am a sane man at this moment. Also, I have seen these things. Much as I know of Kalmarkane's studies, I am not acquainted with his occult methods. The man has power of some kind which defies the limits of ordinary knowledge. He knows infinitely more than other men. Besides, who can say nowadays that anything is beyond possibility? Are there not well-known facts, such as hypnotism, suggestion, evidences of submerged personality, and so on, of which it is out of our power to give any adequate explanation in scientific terms?"

"All this is quite true," admitted Flaxman Low. "But just now, to come to the practical side, what do you propose to do?"

D'Imiran got on to his feet, and his dark face looked resolute.

"I am going back there by the midnight train, because I am determined to get to the bottom of this. But I have told you how matters stand, Low, so that you may know what to do in case I don't return. This is Tuesday; if I am not here by Sunday, I shall be dead."

"I don't think you are acting wisely in pitting yourself single-handed against such a man as you believe Kalmarkane to be."

"Thank you, but I am resolved to go through with it. I have also to thank you for the patient hearing you have given me, and for even seeming to believe me. I shall feel infinitely more confidence now that I am sure, if I lose my life, you will in some manner try to bring it home to

Kalmarkane. I am convinced his power is the result of occult processes, which for want of a better term may still come under the head of Black Magic." D'Imiran stopped and smiled with a satirical twist of the lip. "Black Magic! A couple of months ago I should have sent any man expressing my present opinions to a lunatic asylum."

"To conventional ears your story would certainly sound doubtful," said Low. "But however that may be, the fact remains that Kalmarkane, from whatever source he derives his powers, is dangerous. You are still bent on returning to Crowsedge? Well, good-bye."

Crowsedge is a lonely, plain-looking house built on to a squat square tower of Portland stone. From the highroad a rough track leads towards it over some miles of lonely heath; through dips where marsh and sedge encroach upon the footway, and on across wide ups and downs of dense, wiry heather, where each undulation seems to cut one off more and more hopelessly from the outer world. On the seaward edge of this wild land, Kalmarkane's house rose on the horizon like a stranded ship on a desert shore. At least so it appeared to d'Imiran as he walked over the heath towards it on the morning following his visit to Flaxman Low. Behind the tower crowded rugged sand dunes, and beyond them again, as d'Imiran knew, lay miles of pools and shallows.

With a keener sense of loneliness than he had ever before experienced, he turned and looked back in the direction of the highroad, as if the very sight of its white windings over the downs, suggestive of human proximity and help, might give him renewed courage to face the unclassified dangers which awaited him. But the road had already sunk out of view behind the low ridges of dry heath. For a moment he stopped. After all, was he not a fool to run again the gauntlet of a danger from which he had once escaped? But then came back upon him the determination to get at the bottom of the unaccountable and evil things he had experienced and seen. D'Imiran came of a stiff-necked stock—Huguenot blood on the one side and Ulster energy on the other. So he gripped his bag more firmly, and went on.

Kalmarkane received him gruffly as usual, but gave him a prolonged and searching stare from under his tufted brows.

D'Imiran at once intimated his intention of leaving Crowsedge for good on the following Saturday, that being the date on which his original engagement would terminate.

"As you please," replied Kalmarkane, "I have no longer any use for your experiments."

During the Wednesday, Thursday, and Friday, Kalmarkane kept to his study, giving short fierce orders that he was on no account to be disturbed. On the Saturday morning when d'Imiran came down to breakfast, he found on the table a letter, enclosing a handsome cheque for his services, and informing him that Kalmarkane had been obliged to go to London, and would probably not return before d'Imiran left. This was a disappointment, for the matter of the severed hand still remained unexplained. However, the only thing to be done was to wait for Kalmarkane's return.

D'Imiran wrote a line to Low, and passed the day in packing and making ready for his departure. Next morning he awoke with an entirely unaccountable feeling of depression weighing upon him, which increased as the day went on. In the late afternoon, he went up to his own room, and lighting a fire, prepared to spend the evening there rather than in the dreary living-rooms below. He stood long at his windows; from one he could see the endless moor rising fold behind fold into the distance, from the other dunes and dry sea-grasses, with a faraway touch of red and purple lights defining the salt marshes to the south. As the light faded, a fog slid up from the sea, muffling everything from sight, and rolled in waves close against his windows.

At eight o'clock he went down to the dining-room, where he found a cold meal laid out for him, which he knew of old meant that the deaf housekeeper had left Crowsedge for the night on some business of her own. Dinner swallowed, d'Imiran felt impelled to go to the door of Kalmarkane's study to see if it was fastened. Very carefully he trod the stone stairs and tried the door. It was fast, and with something of relief he came down again and returned to his own room.

He sat drowsily over the fire, dipping into the *Lancet*, but presently he flung the paper upon the sofa, and sat staring into the dull glow of the coals, and trying in vain to reason himself out of his causeless depression. He had furnished his room with a few 'Varsity photographs, and his eyes wandered from one to another as the hand of the clock crept on towards midnight. Presently he heard something like the scrape of a boot on the passage floor outside. He went to the door and peered out, but nothing was to be seen or heard.

Unable to fix his mind on any book, he lay down upon his bed fully dressed as he was, and a sudden sleepiness fell upon him. Judging by subsequent events, he thinks he must have slept for hours, but all through his sleep he seemed to hear a knocking at the door. Again and again, from the depths of a profound weariness, he almost rose to the point of waking—all the while conscious of a vague uneasiness. At length he forced himself awake, and swung from the bed to make up the fire. Then he crouched over it shivering a little, and tried once more to fix his mind on the pages of a magazine. But it was of no use; the words conveyed no meaning to his brain, and he found himself listening to the little vague noises of the house.

Then he began to have trouble with his fire, which waned and smouldered out in spite of his efforts. He took to pacing the room and revolving in his mind the strange incidents he had determined to fathom. But all the while fear was growing upon him. At last with a frantic heartleap he stopped to listen. Some one was softly trying the handle of the door! D'Imiran sat down on the edge of the table. In the silence he could hear the slow drip of the gathering moisture from the eaves on to the broad window-sills. And then came another sound—two stealthy knuckle-knocks on the door.

"Who's there?" called d'Imiran, in a strained voice.

There was no immediate answer; then two other knocks, still soft, but now grown imperious. The very repetition of the noise served to quiet d'Imiran's shaking nerves, and he finally rose, a good deal ashamed of himself, to open the door and see who it was. The lamp was burning brightly as he stepped swiftly and noiselessly across the floor and threw open the door.

Only the hollow darkness of the passage met him. But at the same instant he received a violent upward blow under the chin, which sent him reeling back against the wall, choking and dizzy. His senses whirled, then settled. A throttling grip was on his throat, pinning him against the wall with an increasing pressure. Blindly he flung out his hands to thrust away his assailant, but they encountered only the air! Then he knew what it was, and grasped at his throat in a wild struggle for life.

He was wrenching at those slender fingers that seemed of iron, his head and chest bursting under the fearful strain of suffocation, when a laugh, a long resounding laugh, rang out through the open-doored emptiness of the house. On a sudden the deadly hand dropped off like a ferret from a keeper's hand, and d'Imiran, with an effort that was agony, filled his lungs in a deep breath.

When he came to himself, he saw something lying at his feet. It was the bronze bracelet, with every curve and line of which he felt he was familiar. Then he recalled the laughter; Kalmarkane had returned.

D'Imiran fastened himself in, and sitting down at his desk, gave himself to covering sheet after sheet of foolscap. When he had finished, he put the whole into an envelope, directed it to Flaxman Low, and locked it up in his desk.

It will be well here to give the closing words of this statement, from which the greater part of the foregoing narrative is drawn. After describing minutely the course events had taken since he had parted from Mr. Low, d'Imiran went on to say—

> "And now I can see only one course open before me. I owe a certain duty to myself, and, if I may say so, to my fellow-men. Perhaps nobody, with the possible exception of yourself, may believe my very inconceivable story. Nevertheless, I know it to be true, and I feel it to be my only course to tax Kalmarkane with the things I have here written down. What answer I may get from him I do not know. I can only reiterate my firm resolve that, in one way or another, I intend to try and put a stop to what I think I am justified in describing as the man's devilish schemes. I need only add that I am deeply indebted to you for all the consideration you have shown me in this affair.
>
> "Yours very truly,
>
> "G. D'IMIRAN."

Then d'Imiran rose, his eyes searching for a weapon, but nothing presented itself except a heavy geologist's hammer. Snatching it up he ran through the empty rooms, the echo of his footsteps following him until he reached the tower. A light shone from the study above; he mounted the stairs and pushed open the door.

The room was dimly lit, and there in a high-backed chair sat the man himself, with a hand in his beard and the black stump of a cigar clenched between his teeth. D'Imiran turned the key in the door and walked over to the other side of the table, where he stood among a litter of scientific appliances.

"What do you want?" said Kalmarkane slowly, bringing out the words with an effort, and d'Imiran had time to notice that the great hairy face was ghastly pale. "Earlier in the evening I heard you trying the door. I must own that I expected more honourable dealings from so punctilious a gentleman!" he ended, with a sneer.

"I thought you were gone to London."

Kalmarkane raised his big eyebrows contemptuously.

"Naturally. But as it happens, I have been at work here all day. Now what do you want?"

"Where is that fiendish hand?" burst out d'Imiran. "Twice you have tried to murder me by its agency, and now you are not going to leave this room until you have destroyed it."

Kalmarkane rose, his great form standing stark and upright.

"Vapouring!" he said. "What could you do? It is true that I have tried to kill you, but it was merely by way of experiment. Now, however, if you will answer one or two questions, I will let you go. As for the hand—you shall see me destroy it, because it is no longer of any use to me."

As he spoke he took the hand from its box and laid it in a metal bath. Then he poured out a white liquid over it. And d'Imiran saw the brown fingers contract and twitch horribly as the flesh curled and smoked under the action of the acid. In a few moments nothing remained but a little darkish slime. This again was subjected to the draught of a blowpipe, the apparatus connected with which was unlike any that d'Imiran had knowledge of. Its action was effectual: a puff of dust rose from the bath, leaving its surface perfectly clear.

"If I wished to do away with you, d'Imiran," said Kalmarkane grimly, "you see that I have means at my disposal. Yesterday, that process was part of my equipment of power. To-day, I do not any longer need it. All power resides in the mind of the man who knows how to make his will effectual in the spiritual as in the physical world."

Chilled and shaken as he was, the scientist was still strong in d'Imiran.

"Tell me more," he said. "That hand——"

"Do you ask me to tell you when and how that little hand, full as it was of forgotten treacheries, was hewn off in some prehistoric tragedy? No, d'Imiran, for though you might believe it to-night, you will doubt the evidence of your own senses to-morrow. Now go!"

The last d'Imiran saw of Kalmarkane was the hair-framed pallor of his face reflected in a mirror as he closed the door behind him.

*

"Can you account for his power over the hand?" d'Imiran was saying to Mr. Low during the course of the following afternoon.

"As to that," replied Flaxman Low, "I can do no more than indicate a theory. You are acquainted with the phenomena of moving solid substances which frequently forms a leading feature in spiritual *séances*. The kind of force which is exerted, and the manner in which it is exerted, is still, as you may know, an unsolved problem. When we come to consider the power of Kalmarkane's brain, the years he has spent upon mastering psychical secrets, and his extensive travels in Thibet and elsewhere, I cannot but think that, starting from some such basis as I have alluded to, he may have gone forward, step by step, until he reached to the extraordinary degree of power of which you were so nearly the victim. The weakness and pallor you mention also go far to support the probability of my surmise."

"It may be so," said d'Imiran. "But why, then, did he destroy the thing?"

"Either," answered Low, "he was influenced by your threats, or it has become, as he said, useless to him, because he has advanced to a still higher point of knowledge."

"Can I do nothing to bring him to account?"

Flaxman Low shook his head. "At present I am afraid not," he said. "Some day, perhaps, we may go a little further into many matters with Dr. Kalmarkane."

THE STORY OF MR. FLAXMAN LOW

The very extraordinary dealings between Mr. Flaxman Low and the late Dr. Kalmarkane have from time to time formed the nucleus of much comment in the press. This is partly the reason for the narration of the present story, which may safely be said to be the first true account of those passages which have provoked so much contention.

It has been urged that Mr. Flaxman Low was vastly to blame as the person upon whom lies the onus of the very remarkable termination to the affair.

That is a matter for the reader to judge of when he has carefully perused the facts which we have endeavoured to set forth in the following pages. We have related in the last chapter an account of the one previous occasion on which Flaxman Low was brought face to face with Dr. Kalmarkane's strange influence. This was in the matter of the young doctor, Gerald d'Imiran, at that time assistant to Dr. Kalmarkane, whom Dr. Kalmarkane endeavoured to murder under circumstances which left no doubt in Flaxman Low's mind of the extraordinary powers attained by his great enemy.

It was in the closing days of January that Mr. Flaxman Low, while attending a special meeting of an Anglo-American Society of Psychical Students—on which occasion he read a very remarkable paper on the threefold aspect of the soul as regarded from the ancient Egyptian standpoint—perceived amongst the audience the massive head with its wild aureole of hair which distinguished Dr. Kalmarkane.

After the meeting, Mr. Flaxman Low drove home to his chambers, where some five minutes later he received Dr. Kalmarkane's card. He was a good deal surprised at the proffered visit, knowing what he did of the morose and solitary habits of his visitor. This interview proved to be the first episode in a strange train of events, which directly connected Mr. Low with that formidable and relentless man. Probably it had early become apparent to Kalmarkane that there was no room for Mr. Low upon his path, and that the interview we are about to relate merely brought matters to a head; however that may be, we must proceed first to hint at an extraordinary offer made by Dr. Kalmarkane to Flaxman Low, and afterwards to describe, as far as it is within the province of words to describe, the singular series of circumstances resultant therefrom.

Kalmarkane strode in hatted and cloaked, his stooping, gaunt figure seeming to dwarf the proportions of the room. He nodded slightly to Low, and then his eyes ranged slowly round, as if by the aid of his surroundings to gain some insight into the character of his host. Meanwhile Low recognised the fidelity of d'Imiran's word-portrait of Kalmarkane. "A hirsute giant with a tremendous frame, raw-boned and ungainly. He has a long, strong, fleshy nose, a shock head of dark grey hair, and a ragged beard, which he is in the habit of twisting into spirals as he talks."

As Kalmarkane turned to speak to Flaxman Low, his big hairy hand went up into his beard.

"I have come," he said, "in order to tell you that I was greatly interested in your paper of this afternoon. You have reached a point attained by few before you.—By the way, how old are you?"

Mr. Low, in some surprise, answered.

"Ah," said Kalmarkane, "I am by fifteen years your senior, and I think I may say quite as many years in advance of you in that special branch of knowledge to which we have both chosen to devote ourselves.—Are you sure that we cannot be overheard? I have a certain proposal to lay before you. Let me advise you to give it your careful consideration."

Mr. Low having replied suitably, Kalmarkane went on—

"I came here intending to warn you to draw the line of your studies at the precise point where you find yourself to-day."

"May I inquire why?"

"You have an intellect of a very high order, as well as strength and audacity, and these qualities might hold you safely where you now stand. One step further, the whole aspect of your position changes."

"I do not pretend to misunderstand you," replied Flaxman Low. "But all knowledge is good, if applied only to legitimate ends."

Kalmarkane broke in stormily.

"However we may choose to designate our motives, the final aim of every man is to secure individual power! When you shall have learned the ultimate secret of power, can you answer for yourself that you will never use that power to secure your own ends? Listen! Give me your word that you will reveal nothing of what I am about to say to you, and—and I have no doubt but that we can work very well together."

Thereupon followed in plain but pregnant words an offer to share with Mr. Low the final and immense result of his lifelong toil on certain conditions. Mr. Low listened as his companion flung out each forcible, trenchant sentence, but when he had heard a part of Kalmarkane's communication, stopped him with a deliberate and definite refusal.

Kalmarkane wrenched at his beard.

"Take time to think; for if you now refuse what I offer, neither heaven nor hell can help you!"

"I have decided," was Low's answer.

"This is d'Imiran's work!" said Kalmarkane furiously. "I warn you——!"

"I do not see," said Low, rising, "that we shall either of us gain much by prolonging this interview, and you may be very sure that you are dealing with a man who does not permit threats. And will you allow me in my turn to warn you? You forget, Dr. Kalmarkane, that though there seems no limit to human knowledge, there will always be—as long as body and soul are interdependent—a close-set limit to mortal power."

Kalmarkane swung towards the door.

"I came here entirely in your interests," he said, "and I now add, also in your interests," he ended, with a snarl, "that I do not warn twice."

In a day or two Mr. Low had completely forgotten Kalmarkane's strange visit, being engrossed in further abstruse and deeply interesting investigations on the lines suggested by the paper he had read at the meeting before mentioned. In the course of a fortnight, however, he began to recognise that a new and untoward mental condition was gradually becoming habitual with him, even to the extent of interfering in a serious manner with his hours of study.

Whether its source lay in mind or body was difficult to determine. Mr. Flaxman Low says that he first became conscious of something wrong by noticing that the amount of work he usually got through between the hours of 10 P.M. and 2 A.M. was growing perceptibly less and less, and that the notes made by him during that interval were of a comparatively valueless character. For a day or two he fancied that he must have become sleepy in the middle of his reading, and hence the absence of usual results. The next step was to perceive that at all other times, excepting between the hours named, his work, on retrospective examination, was of normal quality and quantity. Thus it was evident that the attacks of mind-vacuity recurred at regular intervals, and he resolved to watch these intervals.

Accordingly, on the night of the 30th January he placed his books before him as usual, and waited. Almost exactly at midnight he was seized with a feeling of overwhelming despondency, which grew into a condition of resentful frenzy as he brooded helplessly and miserably over some unknown wrong. This phase in its turn passed imperceptibly away, and Flaxman Low found himself reading in his usual manner when the clock struck three, and recalled him to a full consciousness of what his intention had been when he sat down to work. Think as he might, however, a large part of the intervening hours only supplied dim and unsatisfactory memories.

As time went on, these attacks recurred more frequently. The harder he endeavoured to work, the less he seemed to accomplish. His writing began to lose character, many of the letters were slurred; his faculty for close study deserted him, which he felt the more as he was at the time engaged upon some minute and intricate work in connection with a half-defaced Ptolemaic inscription.

At first he was inclined to believe that his health was perhaps to blame for these strange lapses, but in time it grew clear that his mind was at intervals burdened by alien thoughts superimposed upon his own. In other words, he could not concentrate his attention upon his work because he was busy thinking of something else. But what that other subject or subjects could be, he had only a very general notion. His brain was filled with memories which eluded him, memories of some vague and awful unhappiness, a sense of helpless revolt against some crushing fate, but all dim and undefinable.

In the intervals when he possessed himself and could follow out his own train of thought, his position absolutely horrified him, and he resolved time after time to throw off this mysterious ailment by sheer effort of will. For some ten days or more his mental attitude was one of tense resistance, at the end of which time, though physically exhausted, he had in a great measure thrown off his spiritual incubus.

But a further phase of his remarkable sequence of experiences was close upon him. One night, when walking home from his club, he felt that he was being followed. On looking round he saw no one in the deserted street but a policeman at a distant corner. He walked on more rapidly, his pursuer keeping pace with him. He knew those other footsteps fell in exact unison with his own, and that if he could but stop a fraction of a second sooner he must hear them. He hurried on, and shut the door of his chambers behind him with a sigh of relief, which even at the time struck him as ludicrous and unnecessary. Merely waiting to take off his overcoat, Mr. Low sat down at once to work, refusing to allow himself to think over his latest experience.

He believes he was reading when he found himself glancing quickly back to catch sight of the face that had been peering over his shoulder, but he was too late. This happened more than once.

Soon the permanent impression of a haunting presence grew intolerable. Day and night he was never alone, never free from the consciousness of that other intelligence oppressing his own, and by degrees it usurped his thinking powers, seeming to suck from his brain all independent mentality, and to use it solely for its own weird and elusive ponderings.

He knows that he struggled continuously but feebly to rid himself of the tyranny of the thoughts, which were not his thoughts, but those of that hateful personality that dogged him. He always knew that had he looked up, or back, or turned, or stopped a fraction of a second sooner, he must have seen, or heard, or felt his tracker; but he was always by that same fraction of a second too late. On retrospection he now recognises that time after time his intangible companion drove him into situations where by a hair's-breadth only he escaped death. If the reader will for a moment place himself in Flaxman Low's position, and imagine himself possessed by an intelligence determined to wreck him body and mind, he will readily perceive how terrible was a life of which the most ordinary conditions teemed with danger.

Through the long February nights he struggled and waited, set in his resolve to defeat this mysterious influence by sheer, solid effort of will.

At this period there happened to be a sudden burst of bright weather, and Mr. Flaxman Low made up his mind to go over to Paris for a week for change of air and scene, for he was still inclined, during moments of sunshine and activity, to put down his experiences to some physical origin. In Paris he felt better, and often forgot his late troubles. He went out a good deal and saw many friends, M. Thierry amongst others; and, altogether, returned to London feeling fit to face most difficulties that could present themselves.

He attacked his neglected work with fresh vigour and a delightful sense of recovered power. One night he placed his books and papers in order, and made the one other arrangement which always accompanied a long spell of tough work. It is Flaxman Low's habit to fill and place in readiness a succession of pipes in the rack above his head. He apportions them to the amount of work he intends to do, and while his mind is delving in the lore of Egypt, his fingers lay pipe after pipe aside until as many as ten yawn black or ashy from the tray. On this occasion he worked and smoked as usual.

It was long past midnight, and the empty streets lay silent but for the passing of some stray hansom at long intervals. All at once the silence seemed ghastly to Flaxman Low as he stood and looked heavily out of his window. Why he had risen from his chair he could not recall, and the hours since his return from the club had been full, not of work, but of indistinct, puzzling dreams. He knew also that the haunting presence had returned. Never before had he felt its nearness so acutely, nor with the same degree of shrinking repugnance. To-night it almost seemed as if his unseen companion were tangible to the touch, and the perplexing sensation of loss of personality grew upon him as the mysterious presence, pressing closer, usurped the active functions of his brain to brood over some blind, far-off, uncomprehended wrong.

He remembers pushing outwards with his arms as a man might make way for himself in a crowd, and returning hurriedly to his desk. There was a sickly smell in the air, which was known to him, but which he failed to specify. He lit another pipe—the sixth, as he afterwards had reason to believe—and sat down to his work. After that his recollections became intermittent. He was taking up another pipe; dreams and thoughts beyond all power of description were crowding upon him. He was struggling with drowsiness: then he was leaning back in his chair, and eyes were looking down into his own, dark eyes, full of hatred and despair, that carried with them the meaning and the memory of those long, vague, unhappy thoughts: he found himself considering the strange conical cap his companion wore; it was of some woollen material, and thickly covered with short, loose threads, every one of which ended in a knot: then the shadowy eyes, full of compelling hatred, again held his gaze——

Late in the afternoon of the next day he woke to find himself staring at the ceiling of his bedroom, which seemed to sink and recede as he looked upwards. A deadly inertia overcame him, until presently the clock struck five. Recollection began to flow back upon him; he knew he must have slept for fifteen hours. It all came to him now—the beautiful, malignant eyes, and the slender, dark fingers laid upon his brow while his brain swung and reeled into sleep.

By some connection of ideas, Flaxman Low involuntarily looked down at his own hand. Upon his right forefinger was a brown stain. Raising it closer to examine it more thoroughly, he inhaled the same faint, sickly odour that had pervaded his experience of last night. His mind, working sluggishly, hit at length upon the explanation, and the thought sent him reeling from his bed.

Steadying himself by a chair, he looked through a case of drugs which stood beside the door. A bottle of powerful preparation of opium was missing. He staggered into the next room and to the table at which he was in the habit of working. The missing bottle stood uncorked among his papers, half empty.

A horrible suspicion flashed across his mind. One of his pipes still remained unsmoked, and it reeked of opium. Others—the sixth and seventh in order upon the tray—were full of ashes, but the tell-tale odour hung about them still. Mr. Low took up the bottle, and for a moment wonder held him—wonder at the rare strength of constitution that had carried him safely through an ordeal under which most men must have sunk. To a wiry constitution, a clean life, and regular and wholesome habits, he owed the privilege of standing there alive.

After throwing the windows wide, he began to pace the room. He understood now the unaccountable mental lapses of the last few weeks. Some intelligence, other than his own, possessed him at intervals, and taking advantage of the routine of his life and his ordinary habits, had used his own hands to compass his death. He detailed to himself the many escapes he had lately had, and the commonplace events which had led up to them. This brought him to the most important question of all. Who could be the author of so subtle a plot? It is worthy of remark that the possibility of Kalmarkane being connected with it did not at once strike him.

It was at this juncture that Flaxman Low at length acknowledged the absolute need of some human cooperation and assistance. The experience of last night might recur at any time, and the idea that the thing was not only possible but probable sent him once more striding rapidly up and down the floor. He ran over the list of his friends and acquaintances, and he began to be sorry there was so little faith left in the world.

D'Imiran had said something similar. Ah, d'Imiran! The name opened up a new vista of thought. Kalmarkane! In a moment the whole affair became clear to him. Turning to the books he had been using on the previous evening, he examined the marginal notes last written. The few broken sentences bore no connection whatever with the text, but they seemed the echo of those dreams of despair and wrong which had of late worked beneath and independent of his objective consciousness. We may add that these remarkable sentences formed the basis of much subsequent investigation on the part of Mr. Low.

In a very few minutes Flaxman Low had decided on his course of action. First he must see d'Imiran, since d'Imiran was the only man who would believe such strange experiences possible, and was also the only man in a position to give him much necessary information, and perhaps combine with him in the effort he was about to make to shake off for ever the yoke which Dr. Kalmarkane's incredible powers had forced upon him. He looked up the address d'Imiran had given him, and in an hour was hastening thither in a hansom. D'Imiran was in town, but chanced to be out, and Mr. Low left a note for him.

> MY DEAR D'IMIRAN,—If you can possibly manage it, I should like to see you to-night. If you could come over between seven and eight, we might dine together.—Yours very truly,
>
> FLAXMAN LOW.

He walked back to his rooms across the park, and several men who met him on the way remarked that he was looking very seedy.

Once at home, he had nothing to do but to wait for d'Imiran. During the whole of this time he was slowly coming to a conclusion.

"I should have been to see you before, had I not had a very strong reason for staying away," were d'Imiran's first words. "But now that you have sent for me, I am very glad to have the opportunity of meeting you again."

"Ah, Kalmarkane, I suppose?"

"Yes, Kalmarkane."

"He objected to our meeting? For what reason?"

"He appeared to have strong ones," replied d'Imiran, with manifest hesitation; "and it seemed to me that it might be well, both for your sake and my own, to do as he wished."

"I don't know what you may think about that when you have heard my story," said Low. "I had an interview with Kalmarkane about a month ago, and on that occasion he threatened me, and you will, I fancy, agree with me that he has fully carried out his words."

Thereupon Mr. Low narrated his experiences, adding—

"And now you will perceive there is no time to be lost. To-night I go to Crowsedge. I do not know whether you will feel equal to accompanying me."

D'Imiran kicked the fender savagely.

"How do you connect Kalmarkane with all this? He is capable of anything, as I have good reason to believe, but——"

"I am quite willing to tell you what I suspect," replied Mr. Low. "I have told you of the visit he paid me; during that visit he offered to share his secret with me on the condition that I cooperated with him in his horrible schemes. From that time I date my troubles. Let us take the events: my loss of brain-power, my strange periods of possession, and finally my incomprehensible lapse of last night. I believe that Kalmarkane is using some parasite intelligence to prey upon and wreck my mind and body. I have no doubt that if I do not act at once, his next attack will be fatal."

"If you knew as much as I do, I think you would hesitate to go to Crowsedge. What do you intend to do there?"

"My dear d'Imiran, you will understand that there are matters between myself and Dr. Kalmarkane which must be settled once and for all!—On second thoughts, it may be rash to ask you to accompany me."

Flaxman Low rose and slipped a revolver from a drawer into his pocket. D'Imiran, still kicking at the fender, watched the significant action.

"Yes," said Low, in reply to d'Imiran's glance, "it may come to that. At any rate, I am resolved that the settlement between us to-night shall be in one way or another a final one."

D'Imiran's answer was to get his hat. Mr. Low put out his hand.

"I'm going too," said d'Imiran. "I have also, as you know, one or two questions to settle with Dr. Kalmarkane."

The night mail landed the two men at a station not more than six miles from Crowsedge. D'Imiran, who knew the country well, started along the dark road seawards.

The salt wind blew in their faces as they walked on rapidly through the starless, windy night. After a time they left the highroad and struck into a stony track across the heath. Now and then, as they topped a rise, they could see a flashlight far out at sea, but on the land all was black and lonely, and nothing was to be heard but the dry rustling of the heather as the strong gusts swept over it.

Presently d'Imiran pointed to a distant light.

"Crowsedge," he said.

They stumbled on in silence till the thunder of the ground-swell on the coast could be distinctly heard. They were now approaching the house, and d'Imiran remarked that the light was burning in Kalmarkane's study.

They felt their way in the pitchy darkness round to the house-door, which they found unlocked. Then, passing through halls and rooms, they emerged into the lower portion of the tower, where, above them, at the head of the flight of stone steps, a slip of light showed about the door-frame of Kalmarkane's study.

"What do you intend to do?" asked d'Imiran, in a low voice.

"Give him a choice," replied Low, as he mounted the steps.

Kalmarkane was seated at his desk, and looked up with a flare of angry surprise visible in his eyes.

"What has brought you here?" he said. "Have you come to tell me that you have reconsidered my proposal?"

"On the contrary," replied Flaxman Low, "I have come to discuss very thoroughly those other matters that are open between us."

"I have shown you that my boasting was not altogether vain," returned Kalmarkane derisively. "You taunted me with the limits set for mortal men. I have effectually answered you! It is by a mere chance that you are alive at this moment. I am still only learning my powers, but I promise you not to fail a second time. Man, think what you have refused! I have grasped the supreme secret, which has been sought so eagerly but not found; the secret of the Mother-force of nature—cosmic ether! All other forces—electricity, magnetism, heat—are but secondary. I assert that as men have found means to make these secondary forces subserve their purposes, so have I discovered how to control the primal force, for the human Will is above all.

"I have sufficiently demonstrated that I have power, and I can prove that all force is Will-force, acting by and through the vibrations of ether. What are thoughts and emotions but etheric vibrations? And since man can control thought, the conclusion is perfectly logical that he can control the ether. This makes him absolute master not only of the material world, but of those other influences lying beyond its borders!"

"And yet you are only a man," said Low, covering Kalmarkane as he spoke with his revolver. "And as man to man we must deal with each other."

Kalmarkane smiled.

"I give you a choice," went on Low, "I will either shoot you as you sit there, or——"

"Shooting means the gallows for my murderer."

"Possibly, but as the law cannot help me, I must take its functions into my own hands. As an alternative, I suggest that you make a little journey with me abroad, where we can even up our differences as men. This was, I believe, the course adopted by Busner and Wolff, as you probably remember, some three years ago."

D'Imiran has given a graphic description of that scene. Low no longer was the scholar and the man of science, he was the elemental man, ready to abide by the law of the stronger hand. Kalmarkane sat silent, the drops gathering on his furrowed forehead, as he glared savagely at the pistol barrel, which gave Flaxman Low the right to dictate to him.

"You have just sixty seconds to decide in," said Low.

"You have given yourself a great deal of unnecessary trouble," answered Kalmarkane at last. "I will be glad to shoot you when and where you will!"

"That is well; the sooner we start, then, the better, for we don't part, Dr. Kalmarkane, until this affair is finished. D'Imiran will act for me. Pray let me know what are your wishes."

Kalmarkane scowled heavily.

"I have a friend, a Count Julowski, who understands matters of this sort extremely well. He is now at Calais. There is a little cove down the coast there which will suit our purpose admirably," he replied.

There is no need to give here any description of the journey and crossing to Calais, nor of the many precautions taken by Mr. Low. Suffice it to say that the duel was arranged under severe and even murderous conditions, at the express instance of the two principals. The distance was to be twelve paces, and the shots alternate.

On the way to the spot arranged for the meeting, d'Imiran could not control his desire to ask Flaxman Low one or two questions.

"You were able to put forward a very plausible theory in the case of the Brown Hand," he said. "What do you make out of your own experience?"

"There are one or two possible explanations," returned Flaxman Low, "but the one which most satisfactorily coincides with the events is that which I fancy I have mentioned to you already. Kalmarkane appears to have obtained power over some disembodied spirit, whose intelligence he uses to further his own purposes. If you consider the chain of events—my unaccountable depression, the intervals of half-suspended consciousness during which my annotatory writings bore the same stamp of vague desperation, and, lastly, my attempt to make away with myself by adding opium to my pipes—I say if you consider all these things, they certainly point to the probability that a parasite intelligence was acting upon and usurping my mental and physical faculties. This theory covers all the facts."

"But how came Kalmarkane to have influence over a spirit?"

"I am driven to believe that he has discovered not only the secret of etheric energy, but also how to make that energy subservient to the directed will. Did he not boast to you that *all* power resides in the mind of the man who knows how to make his will effectual in the spiritual as in the physical world? Because I believe in that power and Kalmarkane's unscrupulous use of it, I am here to-day."

"If you were aware that he had so much dangerous power," said d'Imiran, "why did you allow him the chance of fighting? I should have shot him down on sight. By your action you are submitting tremendous issues to the lottery of a duel. I cannot think you are well advised."

"One does not readily bring oneself to shoot an unarmed man; and as to his escaping, I hoped, my dear d'Imiran, to render that impossible by the stringency of the conditions under which I had resolved the matter should be decided. He may, and most probably will, succeed in revenging himself; but I can assure you that we will go together, and I do not think that either here or hereafter the death of Dr. Kalmarkane is likely to weigh too heavily upon my conscience."

Such was the conversation between d'Imiran and Flaxman Low as they drove to the appointed place of meeting.

The affair came off in the little cove already alluded to. The gusty breeze had risen to a gale when the combatants stood up between wind and sea. We cannot give any prolonged account of how luck favoured Kalmarkane, who, securing the first shot, brought Mr. Low to the ground, nor of how Flaxman Low, with his bleeding shoulder and right arm dangling useless, fired from the ground, his bullet entering Kalmarkane's brain; nor of how Kalmarkane's great form stood upright for a moment, his finger twitching on the trigger, till he plunged forward, shoulder first, into the sand.

That ten minutes upon the Calais coast has been widely discussed in the papers, and we can only hope that this story will clear Mr. Low from the accusations of savagery that have from time to time been forced upon him. His action in this matter, as in all others, was, we venture to contend, dictated by that high-mindedness which has always formed one of his most prominent characteristics.

It is a somewhat significant fact that at the sale of Dr. Kalmarkane's effects, d'Imiran purchased an ancient oblong box, which was found to contain a bronze bracelet (of which d'Imiran already possessed the fellow), and also a conical woollen cap furred on the outside with little knotted threads.

Of the strange series of experiences in which Dr. Gerald d'Imiran and Mr. Flaxman Low were participators, it is difficult to determine how much may have been due to hypnotic or kindred influences, and how much was naked fact.

Of the secrets possessed by Dr. Kalmarkane, Mr. Flaxman Low can still do no more than indicate the drift. Whether the scientific formula will ever come to light is another matter; at any rate, for the present, the knowledge rests with Dr. Kalmarkane in his grave.

*

In these stories we are afraid it has only been possible to give a very slight and cursory account of the pursuits and character of Flaxman Low. Some day, perhaps, they may be resumed, for who shall say how far his hand shall reach into a science amongst the exponents of which we are certainly justified in calling his the first great name?

Alexander B. Joy is a writer from New Hampshire. When not working on fiction or poetry, he typically writes about literature, film, philosophy, and games. He earned a PhD in Comparative Literature from the University of Massachusetts Amherst. He is the author of *Legend of the River King* (Boss Fight Books, 2026) and a coauthor of *Pandemic Death Discourse* (McFarland & Company, 2025). See more of his work at alexanderbjoy.com.

E. and H. Heron was a collective pseudonym used by the English writers Hesketh "Hex" Prichard (1876–1922) and his mother, Kate O'Brien Ryall Prichard (1851–1935). Hex was an explorer, cricketer, naturalist, soldier, and travel writer. Kate, also an intrepid globetrotter, voyaged with her son to many remote locations; Rio Caterina, in Patagonia, is named after her. In addition to creating Flaxman Low, one of the first modern occult detectives in fiction, the duo wrote stories about Captain Rallywood and Don Q.

Publisher contact:
The MIT Press
Massachusetts Institute of Technology
77 Massachusetts Avenue, Cambridge, MA 02139
mitpress.mit.edu

EU Authorised Representative:
Easy Access System Europe, Mustamäe tee 50,
10621 Tallinn, Estonia
gpsr.requests@easproject.com

Printed by Integrated Books International,
United States of America